*It's heroin. Brian holds the cache in his hand like a pirate grasps plunder. He walks back into the living room with a plastic sack of powder that looks like sifted dirt. In his other hand he's got tinfoil, a lighter, and a small metal tube. A sober silence stretches between us as he lights the powder, which smells like burned barbecue sauce.*

*He teaches me how to chase the dragon, and soon I feel Darkness lifting. It slips away, pushed by a surge of gentle euphoria. A warm flush swells on my skin, a dry mouth, and heavy extremities—like I'm not strong enough to lift my own arm—but I don't want to. I just want to feel it; the calm and the peace, the stillness—even the nausea doesn't bother me. Sleepiness takes me next, and I go on the nod, an alternately wakeful and drowsy state.*

*I'm not sure if it's later that day or the day after, but Brian brings out another fold. His lips draw back as he takes in the smoke. After that, we do it again.*

*I hear people outside his door, hushed voices and footsteps, like ghosts floating in and out, but I don't react, 'cause they are in the apartment next door. I don't care anymore that Mrs. Lieberman has died and that no one else gives a shit about me, because I feel so relaxed and blissfully apathetic, wrapped up in my cozy little cotton ball of heroin.*

*Time is fluid, elegantly slipping in and out of my cup of indifference as the animal in my gut leaves me for a while and I touch peace.*

*It's like when people tell me that everything is going to be okay—this is what it's like; this is "okay."*

*I can't remember eating or drinking or peeing. I can't even remember if we have sex. Maybe it's only the heroin making me feel a gentle orgasm, the absence of fear and loneliness, plus a physical feeling in which all muscles relax. My entire body feels like it's being cradled in a giant, supple baseball glove, or like the feeling of getting into a cool, soft bed after having walked ten miles on thorns with a burning cross on my back.*

*I chase the dragon again, the white curly smoke.*

*Right now, my troubles seem far away, but what I don't know is, they are poised to get much worse.*

# BREAKING
## *faith*

### E. GRAZIANI

Second Story Press

**Library and Archives Canada Cataloguing in Publication**

Graziani, E., 1961-, author
Breaking Faith / by E. Graziani.

Issued in print and electronic formats.
ISBN 978-1-77260-024-7 (paperback).
—ISBN 978-1-77260-025-4 (epub)

I. Title.

PS8613.R395B74 2017          jC813'.6          C2016-906979-6

C2016-906980-X

Edited by Kelly Jones and Kathryn Cole
Design by Melissa Kaita
Cover photo © iStockphoto

Printed and bound in Canada

*Second Story Press gratefully acknowledges the support of the
Ontario Arts Council and the Canada Council for the Arts for our
publishing program. We acknowledge the financial support of the
Government of Canada through the Canada Book Fund.*

ONTARIO ARTS COUNCIL
CONSEIL DES ARTS DE L'ONTARIO
an Ontario government agency
un organisme du gouvernement de l'Ontario

Canada Council    Conseil des Arts
for the Arts      du Canada

Funded by the Government of Canada
Financé par le gouvernement du Canada |  Canada

Published by
SECOND STORY PRESS
20 Maud Street, Suite 401
Toronto, ON M5V 2M5
www.secondstorypress.ca

*To my supportive, loving husband, Nanni*
*and my beautiful daughters,*
*Julia, Alicia, Michaila, Chiara.*
*You are so loved and valued...*

*and*

*To the Faiths I've met and have yet to meet...*

*"You never know how strong you are until being*
*strong is your only choice."* —Bob Marley

*This novel is not only about a runaway teen on drugs,*
*it's about the suffering, bullying and trauma that the*
*protagonist, Faith, has lived through, and why she is the way*
*she is. Only in becoming aware of the baggage that some of*
*us carry upon our shoulders, can we begin to understand why*
*we do the things we do. Hopefully Faith's story will help us*
*to see beyond the "weirdness" as she calls it, and to treat our*
*troubled peers with kindness and understanding.*

# Prologue

The two plainclothes police officers park their so-called inconspicuous black car, get out, and look up at the shabby roof of the town house unit across from ours. Spring rain clouds droop over the city like twisted gray blankets, releasing their first drops just as the pair reach the front door. One of them is young, with blond hair and a buzz cut. The older veteran cop's a little paunchy with graying hair. Both are wearing light jackets, which cover their bulletproof vests.

These images are the first memories I have, vividly seared into my mind, barely being four years old and tall enough to rest my chin on the windowsill. The memories remain with me to this day because I watched the whole thing go down from my upstairs bedroom window.

The young one is the first to step on the landing and is

reaching for the screen door when a discharge loud enough to rattle my window splits the air. A gaping hole is blasted through the front door. One round hits the pane above me and sprays me with glass. The cop with the buzz cut falls to the steps, dead before he hits the ground. I scream as blood trickles warmly into my eye—doors, windows, and shutters begin to slam shut around the complex.

The veteran jerks back, shot in the left arm, but draws his gun fast enough to get a round off through the glass inlay and then throws himself over the railing onto some long forgotten decorative urns.

The shooting stops. I keep screaming.

I feel hands grab my shoulders, dragging me away from the window, throwing me down. Someone lies on top of me, shielding my face. I hear gun blasts and pops and now sirens in the distance.

I keep screaming.

Sinbad, in the house across the street (yes, his name was Sinbad, like the guy who sailed the Seven Seas), firing his semi-automatic at the two cops from the other side of the door, was higher than a kite on crystal meth. Sinbad gets shot right in the chest—at least that's what all the kids in the neighborhood said afterward. I didn't see it, because my mother had pushed me to the ground and had thrown herself over me.

In the following months, I have to sleep with Momma because I wake up with night terrors. Darkness comes over me like a shroud and stays for a long time, and I think I'll never feel happiness again. For a long time, I refuse to leave my mother's side. I have headaches and my stomach hurts and I pee the bed. Momma takes me to a doctor, and he says that I should see a therapist, but it takes us three buses to get there. Momma and I go twice, and then she gives up and says she'll help me grow out of it.

Does anyone ever outgrow something like that? It may ebb and flow, but go away—nah, not thinking so.

I chose to start my story here, because it is the pivotal point, the hinge in my door, the fulcrum in the balance; this is the beginning and the beginning of the end for me.

Look, I'll be truthful. I'm doing this because my counselor told me that if someone is hurting emotionally on the inside that it helps to write things down—it's a kind of exercise, writing about your feelings and fears and stuff. Writing makes you feel better, I guess, because everything is right there in front of you, balls out in black and white.

I guess now is as good a time as any to introduce myself; my name's Faith Emily Hansen, and I'm eighteen years old. I have blond hair and brown eyes. I've got two half sisters: Destiny, the younger, and Constance, the older. And yes, we have nouns for names. I've wondered why that is and I suppose the logical person to ask would be my mother. I do have several theories, into which I have done a little bit of research.

Our names, of course, were chosen by my mother—that was the easy part. Now here is where the research comes in: Constance's name means "firmness of purpose" or "constant in character." And in truth, Constance is stronger than any of us, and is unflinching in her goals, though I would argue that her character isn't as "constant" as I would have liked it to be a couple years ago. But that's for later.

Destiny's name has everything to do with belief in one's future and one's fate. That said, I can see where she has developed the grit to work toward her wishes for a better one. After all, I—her middle sister—was a perfect example of what *not* to be. And in spite of everything, she'll be the first to tell you that she doesn't believe in destiny or serendipity or whatever you call it—she insists that people make their own destiny. And with that, I agree wholeheartedly.

And lastly, there's me, Faith.

*Faith* as a noun is packed with synonyms: *commitment, dedication, loyalty*…. The list goes on. *Faith* brings images of devotion and trust—that is me to a fault. But this is a two-parter. First, faith is a fault when *too much* loyalty and devotion can destroy you if the person or thing that you believe in is hurting instead of helping you. Second, *lack* of belief and confidence when it comes to yourself can really mess with you. I suck at living up to my name with respect to that.

I believe in the deepest depths of my heart that Momma named us after qualities she thought she didn't have, strengths that were necessary to be able to cope with all the crap that life threw at her.

Now, things weren't so bad for her when Constance was born, but by the time me and Des were in the picture, I think she recognized her flaws. Maybe she thought that by naming her daughters after positive qualities, that somehow we would be given the grace to deal with being crapped on, metaphorically speaking of course, in ways in which she could not.

But I'm jumping way ahead now. Let me back up a little and put things in perspective by giving you some necessary family background.

I, Faith Emily Hansen, was born in Greenleigh, Ontario. I was raised in a redbrick row house on Danziger Crescent at the end of Delbert Street, with a blue shingled roof and a green door that had been painted over so many times it was tight in the doorjamb. As a kid, I remember squinting at our house from across the driveway in the worn and weary complex where we lived, and thinking it looked like someone had pieced together giant Legos to create cookie-cutter row houses.

I lived with my mother, Lacey, and my grandmother, Dorothy—Dot, as everyone calls her. We lived as an *almost* normal family until my mother decided that she had some living to do elsewhere, when I was seven, my little sister, almost five, and my older sister, ten.

Then it was just Gran and us three. I'll admit that, at school, I referred to Gran as my mother sometimes, because I didn't want the other kids to know Mom left us. I prayed my classmates never found out, but of course, they eventually did.

"Everything comes out in the wash," my Gran would say. She was fond of using adages like that when she didn't know what else to say.

Allow me to confess that I always knew I was different— and I'm not just referring to the family structure in which I was raised. I mean, my mind worked differently. At home, I would cry a lot because I felt misunderstood and misjudged. And at school, I was a riddle to adults and other kids alike, just as I was a riddle to myself—even with sporadic counseling, I was still weird.

I would blame it on me. Now I know better.

At school, I tended to be morose and sullen and nervous and kept to myself. Contrary to my dark attitude, though, I would often hum while the teacher was in the middle of her lesson, which clearly distracted her. That didn't mean I was happy. I hummed to help myself concentrate because I had too much going on in my head. Of course, she would tell me to stop and would admonish me for it, but I couldn't help it.

In addition to humming, I would sometimes tilt my chair onto the two back legs and fall over onto the desks behind me. The kids would laugh, but my teachers would look worried more than anything else. They would come and help me up and ask if I had hit my head. I would always say yes, even if I hadn't—that was always good to get to go to the office for ice as a distraction.

The office was an altogether different adventure. I had the office all figured out. I pegged the school secretary as a nasty piece of work not long after our first exchange—though now when I look back, she wasn't really. Mrs. O'Grady meant well most of the time. And for the most part, she tended to humor me, unless I tested her patience, and then things got ugly.

Maybe by now people are thinking they know what's coming—my story is the quintessential example of a person who is the sum of all her experiences, and that if I didn't have all these issues, I wouldn't be the strong person I am. I wouldn't be writing this so that maybe it would help out other kids who are messed up. And perhaps others would add that "it's not the destination, it's the journey."

And to this I would vehemently say, "That's a load of shit."

Everyone wants to end up in a good place, the easiest and most effortless way you can get there. Those inspirational quotes are just something people say when other people are having a rough time and they're not sure what advice to offer. Empty words are things I found most irritating when I was on my so-called journey—my journey in the Dark, fighting the demons of anxiety, drugs, and being on the bad side of mental health due to the pain and confusion caused by my emotionally immature mother and a random act of violence.

Often in my "struggle," I felt like what Gran called an old soldier. I don't very much like to invoke the old-soldier metaphor, but in my case, it works well, having lost more battles in my life than I have won.

Like I said, I don't cling much to the power of sayings, but I do have one that got me through most days: "You never know how strong you are until being strong is your only choice." Bob Marley said that. This became my motto when I felt Darkness and fear growing inside me like a cancer.

In my quieter moments of mapping my escape from rock-bottom and dreaming of feeling good about myself, finding the courage and will to talk to someone about the Darkness and my pain is what pulled me off of my own personal ledge. I still need to talk and talk and talk about everything and share my pain, and my talking helps others, and others talk and talk to me and give me their pain, and everything is shared and passed around, and when that happens and other people are carrying some of it for you, the toxic load in your core is lighter.

Call it distraction, call it focus, call it a load of crap, but that worked for me.

And now, as I take strides to maybe someday make the world a better place for me, I realize that no human being, no matter how tattered physically and emotionally, how weary of mind and shattered in soul, is unworthy of our consideration. In my heart, at times when the pendulum swings low, I'm still out there, shivering right along with them.

And I keep writing—this is my ending and my beginning.

# Chapter 1

Her full name was Lacey McKenna, then Lacey McKenna Tingley, and then just Lacey McKenna again. Lacey was my mother. Though she was consistently inconsistent in her mothering style, I knew, for the most part, that she loved me and my sisters. In fact, I always thought one of her deepest flaws was that she made us love her too much.

The summer of my sixth year on planet Earth was an unbearably hot one. It's over a year since Sinbad's rampage, and I still have trouble sleeping because I see the same scene repeat itself each time I close my eyes. Basically, I fall asleep when I'm exhausted, or I sneak into bed with one of my sisters.

My sisters and I all share the same room. It's nighttime and the window is open to let in the humid, stifling air from the outside, to blend with the humid, stifling air inside. Open windows also let in the sounds of the night in our neighborhood, like the sounds from Wheelchair Louie's house down the street; Louie has a steady stream of visitors at all hours of the day and night. One night in particular stands out among the many unforgettable moments in my life, because it's the first time my mom unknowingly reveals that she has issues—and I don't mean regular issues like being over protective or comparing us siblings unfairly or never being satisfied. I mean huge friggin' issues.

• • •

There's a tear in the window screen. It's been there for some time, but the duct tape comes off from the humidity, and Momma forgets to tape it over again—she forgets stuff a lot, and Gran refuses to pick up the slack because she says she's already raised her family and isn't about to raise her kid's family, too.

I'm having trouble sleeping again. My sisters are awake, too, because there's dozens of mosquitoes buzzing around the room looking for the perfect opportunity to zero in on an exposed arm.

Connie huffs out a breath. "I can't sleep."

"Me either," I say. Des shakes her head and continues to suck her thumb.

"You wanna go to Mom's room?" asks Connie, sitting up on her bed.

"Let's tell her we got bad dreams," I suggest.

"It's not bad dreams, it's mosquitoes, dumbhead," Connie

says. She slides her legs over the side of the bed and stands up. I shrug and follow suit.

Constance leads the way, as Constance always does, and pads down the hall, myself and Des in her wake.

Mom's door is ajar. Upon reaching it, Connie's hand goes out behind her, and signals us to stop. She turns and mouths, "Listen." There's a soft but distinct sound—Mom is crying.

I furrow my brow and wonder why she would be crying—does she have a stomachache or is she sick? I don't hesitate. I open the door and say, "Mom?" I sidle past Connie, still holding Des's hand, and walk to the bedside. "Are you crying, Momma?"

"What are you guys doing up?" she asks, propping herself up on one elbow and trying hard to look natural.

"There's mosquitoes in our room," replies Connie, angling her head. "Why are you crying, Mom?"

"No reason," she says as she pushes the sheet off her and swings her feet to the floor. "Sometimes adults just need to cry—for no reason." She smiles as if this should be common knowledge to us kids, but her voice is too cheerful and shaky to be honest.

We weigh her words—our skepticism on one side and the wish to believe on the other. We just stare at her, not knowing what to do.

She breathes in deeply through her nose and out through her mouth several times, then hunches over and whispers to us, "Okay, enough of this. Are you ready to go on a mosquito quest?" Her smile cheers us up, and soon her crying is put on our mental back burner.

"Yes!" Connie says.

"Me too!" I don't know what a quest is, but I assume by Connie's reaction that it will be fun.

"Shh, don't wake Gran." We nod. Waking Gran from a sound sleep would not be a good thing. "We need towels to use as our weapons against the mosquito army." Mom tiptoes to the linen closet and gets a tea towel for each of us. "You start by swatting as many as you can, while I get the duct tape," she whispers.

We spend the next half hour or so swatting the enemy in our room. Mom applies duct tape to the screen, then joins in the operation. We are all extremely silly and loving every second of it. It's one of the last times that I saw Mom laugh from her stomach up to her throat, heartily and completely.

Later, Momma spends more and more time in her bedroom, not eating much, not sleeping; just lying there, being quiet, and staring at the cheap "wheat in the prairie" wallpaper.

Some days are better than others. Momma told us that she was *fine*—I hate that word.

And the Darkness inside me ebbs and flows.

# Chapter 2

Holidays come and go, and we celebrate in our own dysfunctional way. Thanksgiving, Halloween, Christmas, and Easter march into and out of our little house. And with every holiday, Momma puts up and takes down decorations and tries to act happy and normal. Gran remains her usual cantankerous self—though I try to convince myself that she is enjoying it, watching us open our Christmas presents from the Christmas hamper we got from the school. (I figured that part out much later, when I helped fill the same hampers for needy kids as part of a character-building project in middle school.)

Kindergarten at Land Street Elementary is a blur, but I do remember the daily battles of disquiet of what I dubbed the Blood Porch. And I remember the helplessness of not knowing why my mother was sad most of the time and the embarrassment at not being able to let the few friends I had come over because my mother and grandmother were usually arguing. And the feeling of relentlessly being on edge, walking on eggshells, and being guilty for experiencing a positive emotion.

By the time I was six years old and in grade one, the yelling between Mom and Gran was unbearable. My anxiety would peak when they argued, and my mind would relive the Blood Porch incident, making me seek out my sisters for comfort. I found security in snuggling up against Connie until Mom came to us and grabbed us all in a huge bear hug. She made us love her; there is simply no other way to say it. When we were with her, we were all that mattered and we craved her motherly love like a drug. Those were the best times for us. There were good times, but let's just say that they were far outweighed by the not-so-good.

At times Mom didn't come home at night, and this would raise Gran's ire. The arguments would happen the next day, and the three of us heard everything. It was always the same—that's why I remember the fights more than most things.

• • •

It was no secret that my sisters and I all had different dads. Later on that same year, Connie's other Gran decided to take Connie to her house for extended visits.

Connie's dad, Simon, passed away when she was a little kid. Mom's best times were with Simon and Connie. She never said that, but I knew.

Mom used to go into Toronto when we were growing up, though we were never supposed to ask what she did or why she was away—later on, I figured it out. It's bad when a kid figures out shit before the parent has a chance to soften the blow.

"It's not normal, this kind of thing, Lacey—your girls need you at home." Gran's voice is pointed. It's springtime and us three kids are sitting on the front porch, listening to the exchange that floats out to us through the screen door, and I'm trying my best to avoid looking at the Blood Porch. "What do ya think it's doing to them, to know you don't care enough to be here—to see you in the state you come home in, whenever it suits ya!"

"I know you don't believe me, Mother, but I do love my kids." Mom's voice is loud and angry.

"Don't you dare raise your voice at me, Lacey. You've never shown me any gratitude for lookin' after those girls."

"Please." Mom drawls out the word. "Don't you mean money? You don't want gratitude; all you want is the money."

Gran whispers something here that we can't make out, but it must be something bad because Mom starts to cry.

I hear stomping footsteps coming toward the front door. "You come back here and face the truth, Lacey!" The door tears open and then slams shut. Mom pulls a pack of cigarettes out of her jeans with a shaky hand, lights one. She takes a long drag and exhales, then sniffs back her tears.

"Sorry about that, guys." She wipes her face with the back of her hand. "Gran and I just had a little disagreement." She takes another drag and speaks as she exhales.

"Mom, why do you and Gran argue all the time?" I ask. I'm sitting with Destiny on the second step from the top. Mom squeezes in beside us, and Des naturally jumps in her lap. Connie sits on the railing, looking rather detached from the whole situation.

"Because she's just an angry old woman who thrives on spreading her misery around. And boy, like shit in a dog park, she's got plenty to spread around." We all laugh at that. "You know, I think she's just tired and spent and ready to be alone—and we're interfering in her plan."

"Then why do we have to stay here? Why can't you just take us to Toronto with you?" asks Connie. "It's torture when you go."

Mom presses her lips together. "I would love to take you guys there with me. I want to be with you all the time, but downtown Toronto is no place for kids. Besides, my friend doesn't have the space."

"Who's your friend?" Connie's eyes narrow as she asks the question.

Mom looks at the sky. "That's not important." Her gaze finds its way back to Connie. "What's important is that you know that I love you and that I'll be back every week to visit."

"Can you get a friend that has room for us, Momma?" asks Destiny.

Mom smiles. "I'll try. In the meantime, I'm working there to make lots of money for you."

"We don't care about money," says Connie.

"Well, I do." There's an edge in Mom's voice. "I want to

buy us our very own house." There's a pause. We all knew when to stop pushing her buttons.

"Maybe if we knew for sure when we would move there with you, we would be happier," I offer. "When will it be?"

"I don't know." Mom takes out another cigarette, but doesn't light it; instead, she holds it between her fingers and rolls it back and forth.

"Just a guess, Momma. Just a 'guesstimate'—that's what Miss Kelly calls an educated guess." Mom laughs softly.

"Next month?" asks Destiny.

Mom shakes her head. "No, that's too soon." Her voice is soft and her gaze seems far away. After a pause, she turns to us with sad eyes. "Girls, what I'm trying to do is to make myself better—like right now, I might not be the best mom I can be. You may be better off without me for now."

"No, Mom," says Connie. "We can never be better off without you." Connie's right—how can a child ever be better off without her mother?

Mom bites her lip and looks up at us after she's thought a while. She points to where I'm poking the dirt with the stick. "Do you see that?" She's pointing at the burst of color growing out of the soil. "That's a crocus." It is a delicate purple flower, with yellow feathered veins and seeds that look like little pearls inside it. "Next spring, when the crocus grows—that's when I'll bring all of you to Toronto with me to live. Promise."

"When the crocus grows," confirms Destiny.

"Yup, this time next year, when you see that tough little flower peek out of the snow, pack your bags, 'cause you're all coming with me—and Gran, too, if she wants."

"Don't you be making promises to those girls you don't have any intention of keeping, Lacey!" Gran shouts from the kitchen. "You'll break their hearts for sure."

"Quiet, mother!" She jerks her head toward Gran's bodiless voice, then winks at us. Next year, in the spring when the crocus blooms, we will all be together again—a promise is a promise.

• • •

That night, Mom treated us to dinner at Uncle Mario's Restaurant and then took us to the movies to see *Lilo and Stitch*.

After she put us to bed, she went out to visit Wheelchair Louie. I know because I heard the screen door slam shut later on, so I peeked out our window and watched her.

The next morning, she made us pancakes with strawberry faces and then left for Toronto on the afternoon bus.

I cried so hard that night, I woke up Constance. Des was already in my bed, but I needed Connie, too. "Connie, come with us," I said through hiccups.

"But there's no room for all of us," she sighed.

"I'll scoot over—just please come beside me." She conceded to my pleading, and the three of us crammed into one bed. I felt somewhat comforted, albeit temporarily, though it would get worse before it became tolerable.

# Chapter 3

Lacey McKenna, my mom, was a pretty girl in high school. She was the type of girl that boys gravitated toward—long blond hair, slim, and naturally attractive. Once, before the really bad times, she showed me and Des her high school yearbooks. She and my Gran Dot and Gramps didn't have much money, but they got by.

Mom told us about how she went to a dance at Simon's—Connie's dad's—high school. Simon Tingley lived in an affluent area, and his school was in another part of Greenleigh, in the suburbs. They met at the dance and started dating—they were opposites, yet she and Simon fell in love. Before long, Mom was expecting Connie. They decided to keep the baby and get married, despite the protests from Simon's parents that they were only teenagers and should give up the child.

Their little family lived happily for a while in an apartment. Simon worked in the Tingley family furniture business, but one winter day while he was on delivery out of town, a transport truck coming the other way lost control. The highway was slippery, and the truck crossed the median into oncoming traffic, slamming head-on into Simon's smaller cube van. Simon was killed instantly. Mom was devastated. After Simon died, Mom got really wonky—she fell apart, not wanting to eat or shower or even get out of bed.

Mom and two-year-old Constance moved back in with Gran and Gramps, so that Gran Dot could help her look after the baby. Not long after that, Gramps died and left Gran alone, too. Mom met my dad soon after and eventually had me, Faith Emily Hansen—she never did marry my dad. He now lives in Saskatchewan according to Mom. I think Gran didn't like him much, or the fact that Mom had another child. But in spite of Gran's opinions, Mom ended up with yet another baby girl—and Destiny has the same last name as Mom, McKenna. I never met Des's dad.

Connie lived with us and would visit her grandmother—Gran Josephine—on holidays. She always came back with fancy clothes and expensive toys, which she willingly shared with me and Destiny. But when Mom started spending more and more time away, Connie's Gran Josephine insisted on taking Connie to live with her. Mom agreed to it, and, frankly, I believe Gran Dot was relieved.

Connie moving to Josephine's house was one of those subjects that I didn't want to talk about. I yearned to confront her about moving away from us, but the whole topic made me feel awkward. Finally, on the day after the last day of grade one, I worked up the nerve to talk about it.

• • •

Constance and I are on the swing set down the street from our complex, having a contest at who can swing the slowest without stopping. I *must* ask her, so I take in a deep breath, push it out, and the words come with it. "Connie, are you glad you're leaving?" I keep my eyes on the dirt trench that's been carved out under my swing.

"I guess."

"I'm not."

"I know. That's the only thing making me sad about it—you and Des not coming."

"I feel sad, too. More than usual."

"But Gran Josephine is alone. She needs company. And Josephine says that you and Destiny can come visit. I'll make her come get you next weekend, and we can have a sleepover."

"Really? She'll do that? Wow, Josephine is so nice."

"Yeah." Connie nods. "Not like Gran Dot at all."

"True that." I think that expression is so cool—I hear some older kids say it.

"You know, Faith—one night a couple months ago when Mom came home, I snuck downstairs to get a glass of milk and I heard them fighting." Connie looks around to make sure no one can hear. "It was quiet arguing, so we couldn't hear and wouldn't wake up. Gran said that Mom was taking drugs." My heart sinks into my gut. Drugs. I know *drugs* means something bad, though I'm not sure to what extent. The word conjures up all sorts of images in my mind's eye—and they aren't images of the inside of a pharmacy.

"I think Mom is just sad that she doesn't have my dad anymore."

"How do you know?" I ask.

"That's what Gran said."

I'm silent for a while and wonder if she misses my dad, too.

Connie shrugs again. "Gran said that ever since my dad died, Mom has been 'spiraling' and that she's been pulling Gran down with her. She said that she shouldn't have had you and Des—and Gran said that she had to leave her nice apartment and move into housing to get enough room for us all.

"Mom kept telling her to shut up, but then Gran said that Mom needed to leave the guy in Toronto and get cleaned up. To come home and work or get welfare because she needs to stay home and look after us."

I feel like I am going to be sick. I can't speak. *Are we not enough for her? Am I not enough for her?* I can't even look at Connie. The stress of dealing with things a seven-year-old should never have to deal with brings on the Dark feelings again. All I want is my momma and to be safe and know that I'm loved.

Two days later, Connie is set to go. I don't like the idea of my older sister leaving at all—the way I see it, everyone I care about leaves me.

"I'll have my own room and everything, but I'm going to

miss you so much," Connie confides while I help her pack. "I wish Mom could be a real mom and not be so weird."

"Why do you call Mom weird?"

"Because other moms look after their kids, they don't just leave them and go live somewhere else," replies Connie. Lacey may have fooled Destiny and me, but Connie had her all figured out. There was something in Toronto that made Mom feel better than we could.

When we finish, we take the bags downstairs, sit on the living room couch, and wait. Destiny is outside playing on our tiny patch of lawn with the kid next door. Her ball stops bouncing as we hear a car drive up.

"Gran Dot, Connie—Josesine is here." Her voice drifts into the living room, and I smile at the mispronunciation. Somewhat reluctantly, Connie picks up two of the bags and heads out the door. I grab the last one and follow, with Gran coming behind me.

"Hello, Connie sweetheart," Josephine says sweetly. "Hello, Dot," she adds in a crisper tone as she comes up the walk. "Looks like another hot day today."

"Hmph," replies Gran. Turning to Connie, she asks, "Do you have everything, Constance?"

Connie nods, then looks at me and gives me a forced smile. We need to say good-bye but I don't know how. Connie has been my older sister, my companion, my confidante, and my island of normalcy in the middle of this un-normal family. I have too many feelings and they are too big to hold in.

"I don't want you to go, Connie." I hiccup tearfully. "You're leaving, just like Mom." I throw my arms around her and hold her tight. Destiny runs up the steps and does the same.

"Don't leave, Connie," Destiny says softly.

"Stop making such a fuss, girls—she's only a half hour away," says Gran Dot, fumbling in her sweater pocket for her cigarettes. Her eyes are red.

Josephine pinches her mouth in and looks like she is about to cry. "That's right, girls. You can come and visit anytime you want."

"Next weekend, right, Gran Josie?" asks a tearful Connie. "We'll come get them and bring them for a visit, right?"

"'Course, honey, that'll be fine—as long as it's okay with your Grandma Dorothy."

"You can take them all as long as you want." Gran's lips are pursed. She looks away and lights her cigarette.

"Okay, you guys, you heard—next weekend." Connie's eyes are shedding heavy tears. She holds us tight with one more big hug. "I love you, Faith. Love you, Des."

Connie starts to let go, but I can't. When we let Mom go, things never got back to normal, and I know that it will happen again.

"I have to leave now, Faith," she says softly and tries again to distance herself.

"No, I won't let you," I say. Then I hear Josephine's kind voice.

"I'll be back on Saturday morning, with Connie, to pick you up, Faith. I promise." I open one eye. Josephine is on the porch, holding up her little finger so I can see. "Let's pinkie-swear on it." She smiles, and I feel like I should at least give her a chance.

Halfheartedly, I raise my hand and wrap my pinkie around hers. "You promise—next week." I'm extremely serious.

She nods, and her eyes get very serious, too. "I promise, Faith."

Only after I feel that I can trust Josephine do I let go of Connie, and, in turn, Destiny does the same.

My gut instinct heralded the "forever change" as a result of Connie leaving that afternoon. I tried hard to ignore it, to put it out of my mind and to pretend that the feeling wasn't there, but at night it always came back.

# Chapter 4

Josephine did come to pick us up for a visit with Connie the next weekend. We had a slumber party and all slept in the same bed. Connie and I stayed up late and talked about how Josephine had rules—we never had rules; we just got yelled at if we did something Gran didn't like. The next morning, Josephine made us waffles and took us to the lakeshore for a walk. She bought us all matching bracelets that said "best friends" from a cart vendor, then she took Destiny and me home. We all hugged again at the front door.

"See you next weekend," Connie said to us. "Right, Gran Josie?"

Josie nodded. She did come get us again. This time we went to the movies. I loved the weekends with Gran Josephine. But later on that third week, Josephine called and talked to

Gran Dot—she said that Connie had head lice and told Gran Dot to check our heads. Josie said we wouldn't be allowed to go there again until we were "treated." I had had head lice twice before—we all did. The only silver lining to getting head lice in the summer is that you don't have to do the walk of shame in front of your classmates once the nurses check your head. I've been there, and let me tell you: You want the earth to open up right then and there and swallow you whole.

The summer passed with painful slowness and with me, as usual, avoiding eye contact with the Blood Porch. Mom drifted back to Greenleigh during the summer to see us at irregular intervals. She was sad that Constance stayed with Josephine up in Irony Heights and not with us, but she understood the rationale—and she tried to make us understand, too.

Months rolled by like waves on the lake, summer to fall, winter to spring and summer again. I grew up living for the visits from my mom and Connie, and clinging to Destiny as my last connection to family. I rebelled against my Gran Dot (as much as a kid could rebel), after which she would yell at me and sometimes throw things. When this happened, I had learned to threaten her with the possibility of telling on her at school. She didn't like that much, but it did rein her in a bit.

The few friends I made on Danziger Crescent came and went like the months and the waves, our neighborhood residents usually being transient. In school, I became more and more the oddball child, with a detached disposition, hardly smiling, hardly focused.

• • •

In grade five, my last year in elementary school, I learned how truly cruel kids could be to anyone who was different. Until then, being clean or clever had never really mattered much. Not having the nicest clothes didn't matter that much either, but a few months passed and it was like throwing a light switch. The girls became mean and cliquey, and the boys just got dumber.

At Christmastime, we had an especially long visit with Mom, and Connie stayed the entire time. Being all together on Christmas Eve, I felt happy and secure, like I used to feel. Though Mom was looking thin, her features sunken, I pretended not to notice. My heart gave way to the actual feeling of happiness.

I took full advantage of nagging Momma mercilessly about Connie being away, and she tried to explain it to me in terms a child could understand. "See, it's like Josephine is her closest living adult relative besides me, next to Gran Dot. Except Josephine is all by herself, get it?" I nodded my acknowledgment, but deep inside I still couldn't reconcile the fact that she had left.

Before I knew it, school began again, with its lonely days filled with hundreds of children, my glumly disengaged self, warding off even the most well-intentioned child. Without Connie to confide in, there were just too many thoughts in my head taking up space. I had no room to fit math or literacy or social studies in there, too.

Still, I held out hope that Momma would come back home. As early as February, I would dash to the front porch, yet again, and stick my head over the railing as I did every spring. I prayed that I would see the crocus's delicate buds sprouting into the sunshine. Then one morning in March, I saw the tip of its little shoot appearing determinedly out of the dark earth, still surrounded by the last of the slushy snow.

We hadn't seen Mom since Christmas.

"Des!" I screamed and ran back in the house. "Destiny— it's the crocus, it's growing—come and see!"

Des, her face bright, ran from the kitchen and stood on tiptoes to look over the railing. I had done nothing but remind her about Mom's promise for weeks.

"Mom's coming soon!" We danced around the front porch like we had just won the lottery. Hearing all the ruckus, Gran came out to see what had brought on the jubilation.

"The crocus is growing, Gran. Mom said she would come and take us with her to Toronto, remember? Maybe this year she will!"

Gran Dot smiled and patted our heads. "Keep lookin' out for Mom," she said and turned to go back inside.

"Gran, can you call Mom and ask her when she's coming? Please?" Gran looked back at me and then plodded to the phone, with Des and I in her wake. She dialed, waited, and then put the phone to my ear. I listened as it rang and rang. No one answered.

"Tomorrow I'll try again," she said. "I'll call during the day—she may be able to answer if it's earlier." Not being sure what that meant, I just nodded.

"Thanks, Gran," was all I said.

The memories of childhood meld together to form the tapestry of our lives. It is what makes us the people we are, we are told. But are we the product of a string of events placed in chronological order, or are we instead the sum of our reactions to those experiences?

That question has hounded me for years, and I still don't have the answer. Often, I've thought that maybe, just maybe, I don't want to know.

# Chapter 5

That last spring in elementary school, I was especially anxious. I shuddered to think of what my days would be like next September, going to middle school and having older intimidating kids in grades seven and eight around me. I begged the one I called the Ultimate Being to help Gran get through to Mom so that I could move to Toronto, and go to a new school where the kids didn't know anything about me. I figured I could make up stuff about where my dad was and where my sister was, instead of people asking me all the time if it was true that Connie had gone to live with her rich grandmother.

Feelings of isolation were common to me on a daily basis, but the worst parts of the day were the bus rides to and from school. The cool kids from the crescent never wanted me to sit beside them—sometimes they would whisper and pull their hats down over their faces as I walked by, holding Des's hand. Or they would look at me in their peripheral vision and then smile knowingly to the kids in the seat next to them. I knew they were sharing opinions about my weirdness, and I wished that I could scream it out to them, but I didn't dare, until today. The bus ride home that day was another notch on my belt of unforgettable moments in my life.

It started out as usual—shouts, yells, and warnings from Mr. Mel, the bus driver—but I was too excited to care. I was in a rush to get home so Gran could tell me what she had found out about Mom.

Destiny was seated by the window, and I was beside her. Across the aisle sat Jake, at the window, and his sister, Annie, who was across the aisle from me. Everyone on the bus was from our low-income, subsidized-housing complex where there was a mix of people from all over the world. Sometimes Mr. Mel would joke and call us the United Nations bus.

"What are you doing later, Faith?" asks Annie. Her voice has a distinct hint of sarcasm; this in and of itself doesn't surprise me. She is one of the girls who likes to whisper about others when they walk by. Annie has that down to a science. She whispers at the precise moment when you just get past her but are still able to see her cover her mouth and move closer to her best friend's ear, and still within earshot to hear the whispers, which are always mean. I don't think she likes me much, because my Gran once yelled at her mom about the head lice, and not too long afterward, Annie's long red hair had been cut to a short crop. But, despite knowing that Annie blames me for this, I don't hesitate to share my hopes for the evening.

"My gran promised to call my mom today to tell her about the crocus in the front yard. It's growing." I perk up and smile at her, satisfied that I can say something—anything—about my mother.

"So?" she responds with a grimace.

"So, my mom promised that she would come back, no matter what, when that flower sprouts in the springtime."

Annie glares at me with a sarcastic grimace. "Why do you care so much about a stupid flower?"

"It's my mom's favorite flower. She chose it for us—to help us remember that she would move us to Toronto with her soon." I don't clarify that it has been years since she made that promise.

Annie thinks about this for a moment or two. Then her eyes narrow and she goes in for the kill. "My mom says that your mom is doing bad things with men in Toronto. And that she's taking drugs." Her words course from her mouth like searing, burning poison. They settle into my brain and burrow themselves there forever.

I watch her turn her face away from me to face the front of the bus, as if in slow motion. I watch every frame, noting every nuance of her movement. Her short hair bounces against her cheek, and her cheap, ugly dangly earrings clink against her neck. Then I watch her take a deep breath as she sets her eyes triumphantly to the top of another kid's head, straight in front of her.

I can't think of how to respond to her. The callous comments of that ignorant little shit hurt like so many pointed pins being shoved into my cheeks. I can feel my face go red, and the rage seethes in my stomach until, as sure as the sun comes up in the morning, it rises up to my chest and hits the back of my throat—and that's when I go ballistic.

I scream with a voice I don't recognize. It's a scream from way back when people still lived in caves and couldn't verbalize their anger. Then, with equal fervor, I pounce on Annie from across the aisle and slap her with open palms, over and over.

"You mean, ugly, short-haired bitch!" I snarl through clenched teeth. It feels good to say the words, and to let her feel the full force of my fury.

Annie covers her face, and starts hollering for help with screams that are equally primal. "Ahh! Make her stop! She's killing me!" But nobody does. They are all in shock at the ugly scene that is playing out. After a few strategically placed smacks and carefully chosen words on my part, a couple of kids finally move.

"No, Faith!" yells Destiny, her voice sounding small against the bedlam.

"Stop!" Someone grabs my hand.

"Faith, no!" Someone else is pulling my jacket. But I am relentless. Some of the older kids are hooting, egging me on, and others move in to try to pull me off the unfeeling little witch. Then the bus suddenly halts.

"Okay, that's enough!" Mr. Mel thunders. "Everyone stop and sit down—*now!*" I have never heard his voice quite in that way before. Everyone does stop, including me.

"What in the heck is going on there?" he says, unbuckling his seat belt and turning around. "Sit back down, all of you!"

"Faith hit Annie!"

"Yeah, she was slapping her!"

"And she screamed and scared me—"

In the midst of all the finger-pointing, Annie is crying, reveling in the attention she is getting.

"Who was hitting who?" Mr. Mel asks, his voice softer but nonetheless upset.

"Faith was beating Annie up," pipes up one of the older kids in the back. "We tried to stop her, but she wouldn't listen."

"No, you didn't," I say, turning to face my accuser.

"Enough, I said," Mr. Mel repeats. "Faith and Annie, no more. Understand? Hands off."

"She said something mean about my mom." The tears pour out in a spontaneous realization that not only am I angry, but I am deeply hurt.

"You'll have to take it up with the principal tomorrow, Faith—I can't do anything about it now. Just calm down, okay?" Mr. Mel buckles up again and starts for our stop.

Destiny stares at me in stunned silence. I try to hold back my tears and manage to settle down somewhat. Annie continues to lick her wounds, glaring at me every so often until the bus reaches our stop. On the short walk home Destiny and I have to listen to Annie mumbling behind us.

"You're going to be in so much trouble tomorrow," she says as she stomps up the steps to her house, nearly pulling Jake off his feet as she holds his hand.

"Good. I'll sit in the office away from you and all the other stupid people in the class." I flip my ponytail and slam my front door closed behind me as soon as Des is in, glancing with a shudder at the Blood Porch.

"You better leave her alone, Faith—she's mean." Des's eyes are wide.

"Gran!" I shout as soon as I walk in from the hall. "I can handle Annie," I tell Des. "You just stay away from Jake and his lice or we're gonna get yelled at by Josephine next time we visit Connie's." Des giggles. "Hey, let's go talk to Gran and see when Mom is coming to get us."

"Okay!" Des skips along beside me as I mount the stairs. "Gran, where are you?"

A muffled voice comes from Gran's bedroom. "In here." Des opens the door and we both step in. Gran Dot is getting up, her eyes red and puffy.

"Gran, what's wrong?" I ask.

"Are you sick?" asks Des.

"No, I'm not sick." She stuffs a tissue into her sleeve. "Come here, you two. I tracked down your mom through her friend today. I didn't talk to her personally, but she's in a special hospital. They put her in the day before yesterday."

When I hear the word *hospital*, my world turns upside down. "Is Momma hurt?"

"No, not hurt. She's all right—she just needs to get better." Gran looks like she is reaching for the right words. "See, she's sick—a special kind of sick."

"Like cancer?" I feel tears coming again. I know cancer is the worst, so I have to get that out first, hoping that it will be pushed aside. Gran shakes her head vigorously.

"No, nothing like that. She's hurting in the head. Like, she's sad and she took some"—Gran hesitates—"medicine, to make her feel better, but now she's sick because of the bad medicine she took." Now I feel anger.

Looking back, I suppose there is some truth to the belief that there is a defining moment in one's life that you can call the turning point. The second where you can say that an event has affected the way you view things, the way you shape your opinions, and the way you look at humanity. It may also serve to redefine your opinion of yourself and the way you see yourself in the world, the way you believe other people perceive you—or don't. I would venture to say that this was one of them.

"She's on drugs, you mean. And she's doing bad things in Toronto. That's why she doesn't come see us anymore." Tears slide down my cheeks, which I quickly brush off. Gran just looks at me—she doesn't offer open arms to comfort me, but she does roughly take my hand and Des's and pulls us so we are sitting next to her on the bed. I can feel Des's eyes on my face, reading my expression so she can gauge her reaction.

We sit there for a long time. Gran's lack of words speaks for her. Obviously, what I said was true about the drugs and the bad things. And though I'm not too sure about what the *bad things* are, I know that moms aren't supposed to be doing them. Mom is supposed to be here, loving us, looking after us, and making certain that we are safe—like all the other moms do.

"You can't see her yet, but I need to go sign some papers. You're gonna stay with Josephine for the next couple of days.

She's coming to pick you up, okay?"

My heart is aching to see my mother. I can't just let Gran go without putting up a fight. "Please, can we come?" I beg.

"Please, Gran? I miss Mom so much," Destiny chimes in.

Gran shakes her head again. "Can't do it—doctors said not this time—I won't even get to see her for long. They need to have her to themselves for a while before letting family visit. It's best for her. Try to understand, girls."

We managed to get to bed that night, me snuggling next to Des, with a multitude of thoughts running through my head. That foreboding feeling had found me again and covered my heart like black ink. I wondered what the "bad things" were, then I concluded that I didn't really want to know because I might not be able to forgive my mother. Next I thought about not getting into trouble tomorrow, because I wouldn't be at school. After that, I thought about spending time with Connie—that made me happier. My last thought was that at least I could have Josephine's strawberry pancakes for breakfast.

• • •

We've been at Josie's for almost a week. Connie and I are swaying on the porch swing when Destiny asks, "Is Momma coming home?"

"Maybe, but it'll be a while." Connie forces a smile. "Hey, Des, why don't you go and get us all a Popsicle. Red for me."

"Red for me, too," I echo.

Once Destiny disappears, Connie turns to me. The swing stops.

"You really believe she's gonna get better?"

"Yeah. Why not?" *What other option is there?*

"Because sometimes drug addicts don't get better. Once you start, it's really hard to quit."

Her words scare me. "Promise you'll never leave me, Connie. We can live apart, but don't ever leave me." I reach my arm around and hug her tightly.

"You're so dumb." She laughs softly. "How can I leave you? You're my little sister."

Just then, Des comes back with the Popsicles. "Thanks, Des," we say in unison.

"You're welcome," she responds. "And Josie says that once we're done these, we need to get our things. Gran is back from Toronto."

Butterflies explode in my stomach.

The car ride back home is torture. It's all I can do to keep from screaming *hurry up!* to Josie. We pull into our driveway and I can hardly wait for the car to stop, when I tear the door open and run inside.

"Gran!" I shout as I burst into the kitchen. No one. "Gran!" I run upstairs. "Is Mom with you?"

"No, Faith, she isn't." She says from the bedroom. My shoulders slump and I turn to go downstairs, the disappointment settling into my heart.

As I plod down, the others are coming in. "What's going on?" asks Connie.

"Mom's not here, only Gran Dot."

"I didn't think she'd be home—too early," says Josie. All

us kids stand in the hallway and wait, holding our breath until Gran comes downstairs.

"Well. That was a week and a half," she says, surveying us three siblings. I can sense sarcasm in her voice.

"What happened, Dot," asks Josie. Gran shakes her head.

"Lacey's in the rehabilitation facility as of this morning. I dropped her off by taxi from the hospital and then they told me I had to go."

"I thought she was there already," says Josephine.

"She had to detox first."

Josie gasps.

"Well, what do you want me to say. That's why I stayed."

"I know but, do they have to know everything?" Josephine furrows her brow. "A little gentler, perhaps." Gran Dot rolls her eyes and turns to go to the kitchen.

"Not going to sugar coat it, Josephine. What good will that do? They'll find out anyway." The words resound in me. I think of Annie, then I remember that tomorrow I'll probably have to face the music about the bus incident.

Josephine looks at Gran, and shakes her head in disbelief. "Did they say how long for Lacey in rehab?"

"Thirty days. Then real life kicks in and she has to rejoin the world again."

I think about what that meant. Why did Gran Dot always speak in riddles? Was she coming home in thirty days? Rejoin the world? I'm confused.

I hated saying good-bye, but it was time. Connie, myself and Des all group hug, but it is hard to let my big sister go with all these questions in my mind. I want to talk to her about *rehab* and what it means for us and for Mom and what she thinks. I want someone to tell me that it's going to be okay and that Mom will be better forever.

"I'll call you tomorrow." I whisper to Connie. She nods and squeezes Des and me.

"Bye girls," says Josephine. "We'll see you again real soon."

But soon was not soon enough. We wouldn't see each other again until Mom was released from hospital.

In the meantime, I knew that Gran had no idea about what happened on the bus—we left in too much of a rush that day for her to ever get the phone call. I had to tell her about the fight with Annie before the school did and I was not looking forward to that.

# Chapter 6

"Do you know why you're here, Faith?" asks Mrs. Fargo, our vice principal. I don't offer any information. It's the first day back at school since returning from Josephine's, and I'm in the office by recess time. Everyone ignored me on the bus, but I like it that way.

"Did something happen on the bus between you and another student last week that you want to tell me about?"

I shake my head with the most innocent look I can muster up.

"Faith. I know what happened on the bus."

*Then why are you asking me?*

"I also know that things have been happening at home that might have sparked this behavior. You need to understand that what you did was unacceptable. But I understand why you did it."

I look up, surprised.

Mrs. Fargo leans her elbows on her desk and speaks softly. "I talked with some of the kids on your bus, and they tell me Annie has been giving you a hard time about your mom."

I try hard to suppress it, my eyes begin to sting and brim over with tears. I simply nod back to her.

"I thought so." The corners of her mouth warm into a smile. "I spoke with your grandmother this morning, and she agrees that it may be best if you speak with someone about what's happening. Is that okay with you?" I nod again. "A counselor will be in this week to talk with you about whatever you want—your mom, sister, any questions about where your mom is—you decide."

• • •

Two days later, I'm called down to the office again. It's during math period—this, in and of itself, is a welcome happenstance. Mrs. Fargo meets me at the door and motions me into her office.

I walk in and am shocked to see my grandmother sitting with a pretty lady at a round table. Seeing Gran in the school is weird. She never even comes to parent-teacher interviews.

"Faith, this is Shelley," says Mrs. Fargo. "She is the counselor I told you about."

The pretty lady has a genuine smile that shows off her perfect teeth. "My name is Shelley Hazen and I work for the school board. It's nice to meet you, Faith." Her voice is soothing and soft. "Your grandmother and I have already had a conversation about what's happening at home. Sounds like you've had a rough year."

I look at my Gran. She nods to answer. "Yes," is all I offer.

There's a pause and Shelley licks her lips. "You know, Faith, sometimes when we're confused or don't understand what the adults around us are going through, we feel afraid and over-whelmed. Often that fear makes us sad. Now a little sadness is okay; it's an emotion just like happiness, worry, or anger. But too much sadness can be a harmful. Do you follow me so far?" I nod and look at Gran. She seems bored.

"All right, then—why don't we start off with your mom. You know she's been in Toronto for a while, right?"

"Yes."

"And your Gran tells me that you know where she is right now, in a place that will help her get better."

"She's in a rehab center because she's addicted to drugs." It comes out rather bluntly. Shelley looks at Gran.

"I don't believe in sugarcoating the truth."

"That's pragmatism for you." Shelley smiles. Gran doesn't smile back. The counselor's attention turns back to me. "Do you have any questions about how they are going to help your mom get better?"

"Yes. What do they do there?"

"Well, there are doctors and nurses and therapists there who are taking care of your mother's health and well-being. They will treat the drug addiction and ensure that your mom gets better physically, and they'll make sure she receives care for anything else that may be bothering her. That is the best way to help her to get well, and stay well."

"Can she come home after she gets out?" I brighten a bit.

"That's up to the doctors," says Shelley, "but I'm sure you will be able to see her soon, right Gran?"

Gran nods. "Are we done here?" She stands up.

"Ah, yes, but I'd like to have another word or two with Faith, if you don't mind."

"'Course not." Then she turns to me and holds up her warning finger. "No more fights on the bus, understand?"

"Can I just see you outside for a moment?" Shelley says as she follows Gran out. She closes the door behind her but is only gone a few minutes.

When she returns, she has two Popsicles. "Look what I got from Mrs. O'Grady." She smiles warmly. "Which one, blue or red?"

I choose red. We slurp our ice pops for a moment or two, then she begins to talk again.

"Before you go back to class, Faith, I need you to understand two very important things. The first thing is that even though sometimes the adults around us don't show us that they love us, they really do." I know right away that she's referring to my grandmother. "The second thing is that children do not cause or create the problems adults have in their lives—now I'm talking about moms, dads, grandmothers—any adult." Though I know Shelley is appraising me, her eyes show compassion. "Grown-ups are responsible for their actions, good or bad, not their children."

"You're talking about Mom and Gran?"

"Sort of, but mostly I'm talking about you. I don't want

you to blame yourself or think that you or your sisters may have been the reason why your mom has a drug problem. You're kids and you deserve to have a responsible adult look after you. It's not your fault; don't ever forget that, okay?"

Listening to her telling me that I deserve to be taken care of makes me feel better. The Popsicle helps, too. "Okay, Shelley." I swallow the last bit of my Popsicle.

"Can I come back and see how you're doing next week?"

"Sure." I look away, unsure how to react.

She gently takes my empty wrapper and tosses it into the garbage. "Promise me one thing. No more fights. Hands off. There is never an excuse for violence."

"I promise." I leave the vice principal's office feeling better than I have in weeks.

• • •

March crawled by, even with the much anticipated spring break after the long, cold winter. But the day finally came when Gran had to go to the rehab clinic in Toronto to get Mom.

"Today's the day!" I squeal all the way downstairs to the kitchen, where I grab Des's hands and twirl her around. She giggles and dances with me.

"Okay, settle down. Don't do your happy dance yet. Your mother still has a long way to go before you can celebrate," says Gran, tucking a sandwich in her purse. "She's outta the clinic there, but she's still gotta go to the outpatient clinic here."

"What's that?" Des asks.

"It's when people like your momma go to the special clinic

only during the day and hope that they don't fall into the same damn trap with drugs after they're cut loose from the hospital. Which is a pain in the ass for me 'cause I gotta go with her to some of these sessions."

"But you're happy she's coming home, right?"

"I should be." Her face looks a thousand miles away. "But at least there, I know she's away from people who might lead her down the same road again. Here, she's gotta be strong on her own."

"I'll help you, Gran," I say, scrounging in the fridge for bread and Cheez Whiz. "Please be nice to Momma. Don't fight with her, okay? Please."

Gran's mouth starts to work. She sucks in her lips and bobs her head up and down. "I'll try," she says softly.

• • •

Shelley and I talk again that day. She sits at a table in Mrs. Fargo's office, and I sit across from her.

"I hear this is a big day for you and your family, Faith. How nice to have your mother home again. How do you feel about it?"

I shrug. "I'm glad, I guess."

"Just glad? Aren't you excited to see her?"

"Well, I was really happy to see her this morning." My voice is thick with emotion. "But then Gran s-said that i-if sh-she comes h-home—" I start to hiccup uncontrollably. Shelley reaches over and pats my shoulder. "She m-might end up t-taking drugs again because sh-she is in the out-outpatient hospital." Another cry escapes from deep inside. "And sh-she was supposed to c-come back when the crocus bloomed in our f-front yard, but she never did."

A tissue brushes up against my cheek. "I'm so sorry, Faith. Here, honey—take this." Gratefully, I accept the tissue and wipe my eyes and nose as Shelley waits patiently for me to get myself together.

When my hiccups subside, she speaks. "Feel a bit better now?"

"Yes," I lie. My outburst makes me feel ashamed.

"Good." She smiles at me and reaches across the table to squeeze my hand. "Well, I don't know anything about a crocus, but first and foremost, it's not up to you to take care of the adults around you or feel guilty because they need to take care of you—that's their job. They are the adults, not you." She pauses.

"I know your Gran must be happy that your mom can come home, but I think she's probably scared, too, just like you."

I nod and try to understand. Listening to Shelley makes me feel calm, like everything is going to be okay—I crave that calmness of spirit. Abruptly, I rise from my chair and dash around the table to throw my arms around her neck. She hesitates for a moment, then hugs me back, albeit for an instant, but she hugs me back.

• • •

Destiny and I grow more excited the closer we get to our stop. As we round the corner to enter our street, I see Momma, arms crossed in front of her, pacing up and down the pathway. She's thin and has shorter hair, but it's her!

"Look, Des, it's Momma!" I yell out.

"Where, where? I can't see!"

"Just there!" I point over the kid's head in front of us. Des stands up but is too short. The kids in the bus are smiling, too—I think they're genuinely happy for us today.

"Sit down, girls—almost there," says Mr. Mel.

I never take my eyes off Mom—her hands are up to her mouth and she's laughing and waving at us from the curb. As soon as the bus stops, I grab Destiny's hand and hurry to the front door.

"Thanks, Mr. Mel!" We tear down the steps, through the doors, and into Mom's arms, Des and I both. She kneels down to hold us, and we just throw ourselves into her, laughing and crying. I bury my face in her hair. She smells wonderful; the smell of comfort and safety, of home and love. I sparkle inside.

"My babies, my babies…oh my God, I'm sorry, I'm sorry—I'm so sorry," Momma sobs. She holds us tightly and cries into our jackets for what seems like forever, as she rocks us back and forth. Nothing can hurt me, no one can make me feel bad because Mom is holding me.

Then slowly we detach. Momma looks healthy and rosy-cheeked. Her loving gaze caresses me and Destiny, trying to take in every detail in our faces that may have changed in the months since she last saw us.

"I can't believe I'm home." She tenderly tucks our tear-dampened hair behind our ears and then reaches up to touch Destiny's forehead, and then mine, with her lips. "I love you guys so much and I'm so sorry. I just can't say it enough." Her face is home. I feel peace, calm; no anger, no resentment, no Darkness.

"I missed you, too, Momma." All I want is for things to be good.

"Me too," chimes Des. Her little voice quivers as she brings her arm around Mom's neck and gives her another hug. I let my head rest on Momma's shoulder as long as she will have me there. Then she begins to stir.

"Okay, my beautiful babies—I'm going to stand up now. Here, give me your hands." We slip our hands into hers and start walking, clinging to her like we will lose her. We walk to our house at the end of the lane, never taking our eyes off her. Even the Blood Porch is forgotten today.

Still, I know that there will be time for hard questions and deep emotions later. Time to ask, time to cry more, time to grieve for moments lost, and time to forgive, but this is the time to be happy. As we get closer, I see Gran's face framed against the screen door, giving way to a smile.

# Chapter 7

Josephine brought Connie over that same afternoon, but a much different scene played out in our front hall than on the curb of Danziger Crescent. Connie was polite but cool. She gave Mom a cursory hug, then turned to Des and me and gave us both a huge squeeze.

"Hi, guys—missed you," Constance whispers in our ears. She is in grade eight now and is looking totally like a young woman. She takes her jacket off and throws it on the hallway bench.

Josephine follows Connie, holding a casserole dish and wishes Mom well, but she looks tense. Only the Ultimate Being in her infinite wisdom knows what's going on in Josephine's head at this moment. She could be wondering if she should trust bringing Connie, her only grandchild, back to her drug-abusing daughter-in-law's house. She could be thinking that the best thing would be to just grab Connie and run like hell away from us. Maybe she's worried about the effect of all this on Connie, like I'm hoping my Gran is worrying about me.

"I brought a lasagna, Dorothy," says Josephine as she and Gran Dot enter the kitchen. "I figured you could use it."

"I'll take all the help I can get," Gran responds, taking the casserole dish.

"Okay, girls." Momma puts her arms around our shoulders. "Let's sit a bit and talk, catch up, while the grans are in the kitchen." She guides us into the living room, where we wait for her to start the chat.

Mom looks intensely uncomfortable. After the initial euphoria of the reunion, all our thoughts are focused on the proverbial elephant in the room—her substance abuse and ensuing absence. I wonder how we are going to start, but Destiny takes the lead.

"Mom, you're not going to leave us again are you?" she blurts out. I feel a collective sigh escape Connie and me.

"Oh God, no!" Mom sputters. "No! I will never leave again." She pauses. "I'm going to work really hard, now that I'm back, to be a good mom for you, be the mom you girls deserve."

"What were you doing, Mom?" Constance's face is pragmatic and unyielding. "Why were you gone? Tell us so we know, right from you, from your own mouth."

Mom sits up really straight and sighs. "I'm a drug abuser. And alcohol sometimes, too. That's all you need to know about that. I will tell you that I used them at first because they helped me to feel better. But after a while, not having them hurt me even more than what I was missing." Her tone is raw, honest.

"I'm glad you're back, Momma. I don't care what you did—just don't go away again."

. . .

Dinner is awkward by anybody's standards. Talk gets around to how Josephine will take Connie back to her place, so that she can finish out the week at her school and then come back home to us for the weekend. Mom doesn't look thrilled.

"Connie, why don't you stay over—we can all stay together in the same room tonight and just talk," begs Mom.

"I can't. I have to go to school tomorrow—I have an important performance task on my math unit to finish."

"And you have to go to the clinic tomorrow morning, too, Lacey," Josie reminds Mom.

Mom slams her knife and fork on her plate. "You know, Josephine, Constance is still my daughter! *My* daughter." Her lip is quivering.

Gran takes in a deep breath and sips some water. "Oh shit," she murmurs. The rest of us freeze and wait for it.

Josie sets her knife and fork down, then wipes her lips with a serviette. "Lacey, when you began your life in Toronto, I took in Connie, not only to make things easier for Dorothy, but because she is *my son's* daughter. Simon would have wanted me to bring her home—to my home—because I'm the closest thing she had to a father *or* a mother when you left—"

Connie holds out her hand to stop Josie. "Wait, Gran.

Mom, I think what Gran Josie is saying is that even though you're home, I can't just drop everything and come back. I'm in grade eight now, I've been at that school for years, I've made friends, I'm on the student council, I graduate this year, I—"

"Okay, okay." Mom breathes out as her face flushes. "Connie, you take as long as you need. I don't want to upset your life more than I have already. That just wouldn't be fair, or realistic. I was just hoping that…that we could…"

"We will, Mom." Constance smiles weakly and casts her eyes on me and Destiny. "We will. I need a little time is all." She wipes her mouth and sets the rolled-up serviette on the table. Destiny looks to Mom, then Constance. "Are you coming back, too, Connie?" It's so easy for Des—simply come back, like nothing's happened. A child's innocent mind, thinking it could all go back to the way it was—or the way we thought it was.

Oddly, it's what Mom was expecting, too.

At the door, our good-byes are strained. Connie is cold to Mom, but hugs Destiny and me with all her heart and soul. I can smell her guilt at leaving us, but I can also see that her desire to go back to her affluent life in the suburbs outweighs the benefits her sisters would reap from her presence.

# Chapter 8

Mom has made it through three weeks of outpatient rehabilitation. She's doing well, I think, encouraging myself that everything's finally going to be okay. Then Connie drops the bomb—she's staying with Josie indefinitely.

Social services got involved, but it was decided that there had been enough trauma and harm done in the relationship, so it's suggested to Mom that perhaps it's best to wait it out and let Connie heal in her own way.

"Connie, you promised," I beg her over the phone. "You promised me you wouldn't do this. Come home. Momma needs us around her."

"Faith, I love you, but I'm sick of talking about what Mom needs. What about what I need, or what you need, or Des… what about that? Did you ever think of that—does *she* ever think of that!"

For this, I don't have an answer.

Connie's decision is as devastating to Mom as it is to me. But what I don't realize is Mom is weaker than I thought.

One night I hear Mom and Gran's angry voices downstairs. I pray to the Ultimate Being that Gran will stop talking to Mom in that way. Filled with curiosity, I go to my door and open it just enough so I can hear better, but by that time the conversation ends. The final words are punctuated by a slamming door and then quiet.

My mind is stewing over what they could have been talking about—was it me? Was it Connie? Of course, it had to be Connie. She was the one causing trouble—she wasn't helping Mom at all by staying away. All she was doing was making it worse by leaving. I feel the Darkness creeping back into my belly, spreading inside me like a choking fog.

And who left—was it Gran going out for a cigarette and to drink her tea, or was it Mom? And if it was Mom, where did she go? And if she went, was she coming back? *This is all Connie's fault.* My mind is creating scenarios of the possibilities, each one a Venn diagram of conjecture and possibilities of blame through endless variables and contingencies. I scooch over next to Destiny and hold her tight, hoping it will ward off the gloom.

In my mind, it is everyone else's fault but the one in the center of the Venn diagram—my mother. Eventually, sleep finally comes and allows my mind some much needed peace.

The next day, I am awakened by Mom. "Get up, Faith, sleepyhead." Des is in the washroom, water is running, and

Des is singing. I get up and get ready for school, go downstairs to breakfast. I note that Mom's eyes are red and she's got the same clothes on from last night. I sit beside Destiny and reach for my orange juice.

"Did you go out last night, Mom?" I ask, looking up from my toast. I don't want it but I think that I must eat it or I'll stress Mom out. My mind races.

"I did." She sits beside me at the table and nibbles on a piece of my toast. "I needed some cool air—to get away from your grandmother's hot air."

I laugh softly. At least she still has her sense of humor. We pause after the joke and then we get serious again. Her eyes are hollow, and I don't know how to comfort her.

"Don't cry about Connie anymore, Mom—she'll come home." I reach over and squeeze her hand. "She promised me she would."

"I hope you're right." She squeezes back. "I can't blame her—and neither should you." I can't help it—I blame her for that and more. A moment of silent reflection is interrupted by Mom's cell phone. She answers.

"I told you not to call me here," she says as she peers at me with her peripheral vision and skulks out of the room. "I wasn't answering my cell because I didn't have it on me…"

I creep to the hallway door to listen. "No, you can't come here…well, Louie shouldn't have told you, that asshole…no! I…"

I take a step closer and the floor lets out a huge creak. Immediately, she stops the conversation. "You and Des better hurry or you'll miss the bus." She runs up the stairs, closing her bedroom door behind her.

All appears to go as usual for the next week, and then the dominoes begin to fall.

One night, after Destiny and I go to bed, I hear Mom mumble something to Gran. Gran says something back, after which I hear the door rattle open and shut. Unwilling to let myself drift off to sleep without investigating, I creep out of bed and pad to the window. It's Mom and she's on her way to Wheelchair Louie's house.

My mother had reached a fork in her road that week. The unwillingness of Constance to move back home with us, coupled with the stresses of battling familiar influences and temptations while outside the cocoon of inpatient counseling, pounded on Mom like a hammer to butter. The downward spiral happened outside of my awareness. I figure that she stopped going to counseling at about the one-month mark, not long after she had tread the familiar path to Louie's. And when her "friend" from Toronto came to collect her, it was too easy for her to surrender.

She couldn't stay away from the bad man who made her feel good. He came to claim her because he knew she was weak enough to let herself be persuaded and it was easy for him. Lacey McKenna Tingley left us, her children, and the last chance she would have had to make things just a little right for us all on a Thursday morning—when we were at school.

• • •

I see Gran at the bus stop. I step down behind Destiny. "Hi," Des says to Gran.

"Where's Momma?" I ask. Since she's been home, she's met us at the bus every day.

"Let's go home—we can talk there." A wave of doom washes over me like dirty water. The short walk to the house seems to stretch endlessly in front of me, like in the movies, where people are running to a door, but it gets farther and farther away. Destiny chatters to Gran, but all I hear are muffled words as everything around me seems to hush and my ears begin to ring. Blood Porch is on my left and Gran is on my right and I see nothing ahead of me.

When I step inside the house, I see Josephine with her arm draped over Connie's shoulder. My sister, eyes red and wet, and tears rolling down from her chin to her uniform skirt, looks up as I stand on the threshold to the living room. I feel them staring at me and Des as we try to come to terms with what I suspected as soon as Gran opened her mouth at the bus stop.

"Faith, Des…" Gran's mouth tries to work, but even she can't bring herself to tell us. "I called Josephine earlier and told her about it…and she brought Connie down—so you three could be together."

"Is Mom dead?" I ask, feeling like someone has to say it.

"No. She's alive," Josephine says. "It's not that…. Girls, your mom had to go." Her tone is soft and gentle. "She left for Toronto."

"No." I say. Like if I say no, it's not going to be true.

Destiny walks over to Connie. "For today?" I know the

answer to that. If it was only for the day, there wouldn't be such drama. She must have made it clear that she had no intention of coming back—for crissake, it was like it was her funeral in that room.

Josephine looks up at me from her spot on the couch and speaks. "No, honey. She said she was moving back. It's not because of you girls." She casts her eyes downward, looking for the words that would hurt us the least. "I think she may have relapsed." Her lips become tight. "She told Gran Dot that she was staying there. She couldn't face you, but she said she would call you later on and try to explain and that she loves you very much. I'm so, so sorry."

Destiny begins slowly, then lets out a guttural wail. She grabs on to me and I wrap my arms around her—but I feel nothing. Connie has resumed shedding tears. *That two-faced hypocrite. What the hell is she crying about? Connie never wanted anything to do with Mom after she came back. She made Momma believe that her oldest daughter hated her and now she's crying 'cause Mom left?*

"What's your problem, Connie?" Contempt for my sister boils inside me. "You're why she left—because you wouldn't come back!"

"What are you saying!" wails Connie. "She didn't leave because of me." Destiny clings to me so she won't drown in this latest installment of our family's *Titanic*-like reality.

"'Cause of you! 'Cause of you!" With words barely intelligible, I accuse her again and again of having been the instrument of Mom's latest failure. "You didn't wanna come back! She tried so hard to be good, and she came back but you didn't." My eyes turn to Josephine. "And you helped her, Josephine!" Connie stops crying and takes on a look of disbelief with a little sanctimonious resentment thrown in.

"No, Faith—it's not Connie," Gran Dot says quietly. "Or Josephine or you or Destiny or even me. There's no one to blame here but your mom." I whirl around to face my grandmother and can't catch my breath because everything she said was evil and cruel and I hate her.

"You did it to her, too! You always yell at her and say things that make her feel like she doesn't belong here! Why can't you be like other grammas!"

"Stop it, Faith!" cries Des.

"Yeah, you're upsetting her, you stupid little shit!" Connie stands. "And stop sticking up for Mom—*she* is doing all this. *She* is, not us—because she can't say no, she *cannot* say no to… to the drugs or that…that piece of shit guy who's giving it to her." Standing silent, I never take my eyes off her as her words churn out like so much sewage.

The truth, the whole truth, and nothing but the truth— and Connie has just laid it all out for me in a clear and concise few sentences.

Perfect.

I look down at Destiny, who's still clinging to my waist— her wailing has ceased. We're all in the living room, just breathing, looking at one another, waiting for the next person to speak up, but nobody does.

"Destiny, I'm going upstairs. Come with me." I take her

hand and stomp up the steps, Des trailing behind me like a puppy dog.

"Wait!" cries Constance. "Faith! Wait, don't go." I hear her footsteps not far behind me. "I'm sorry, but it's true."

I round the doorway into our room, clear the crap off my bed, and flop facedown, with Destiny bouncing up beside me. Then I hear Connie's footsteps stop at the doorway.

"Faith, come on. You had to know." Most of the anger in her voice is gone and is replaced with an urgent tone. "You had to suspect that there was something going on."

"Leave her alone, Constance." Gran's voice floats up from the living room. "How is she supposed to know; she's a child."

Silence for a few moments, then I hear, "Faith? Destiny?" The bed bounces again. My ears pick up footsteps walking to Destiny's bed, squeaking springs and the noise of ruffling blankets. I hear low voices coming from the living room—it sounds like Gran and Josephine are having a sit-down, too. I peer up from my pillow to see Connie and Des comfortably cocooned under Des's covers. I'm shivering and I so long to be comforted.

A battle of wills begins to wage in my mind—shall I let go of my pride, join them, and feel better, or should I fight for my self-satisfaction and stay? I puzzle about it for a long moment, but there comes a time when you're willing to forget anything your stupid sister has said, to reassure yourself that you are part of a greater thing than your own self-importance. So I do the logical thing—I crawl under the covers with the people on Earth I love the most.

• • •

I won't bore you with details. Just know that our encounters with my mother from that day on were sporadic and inconsistent, and each time we saw her, which was weird because we always had Gran or someone from social services with us at every visit, she begged forgiveness and couldn't stop kissing, hugging, and telling us how much she loved us. She looked much thinner and older than her years. Sometimes Connie would come, too, but mostly not.

I always told her that I loved her back, and so did Destiny, but the anger and hurt never went away.

# Chapter 9

When Shelley and I talked over the next few months, it felt like she was all mine—like she was there for me only. Shelley would talk to me about school stuff and home stuff, but mostly my feelings and my anger. She explained to me that we all have anger inside us.

"You know, Faith, anger, really strong anger, like you felt on the bus that time and the anger that makes you hit others, is a sign that something is wrong—that you are hurting deep inside. Anger is a response to pain, Faith, and we don't want to ignore that or minimize it—do you understand what I'm saying?"

"I think so."

"Anger is a natural emotion—it's okay to be angry. We get angry because sometimes life hurts, but if you handle that anger in an inappropriate way, then that is when you cross the line—you know?" I nodded. "Why don't you tell me again what I said, so I'm sure that you know."

"It's okay to feel mad because it is a feeling like being happy is a feeling, but we can't use being mad as an excuse to hurt people."

She raised her hand palm up, and I gave her a high-five. "Perfect," she said. "Anything else you want to talk about?"

I thought for a moment. "Oh! We have a cat now. Gran let us keep this stray cat that Des and I have been feeding the last couple weeks. She says it might help us feel better."

Shelley smiled her beautiful smile at me, and I felt lighter.

Of course, once I got back to my classroom, they began to tease me about being in the office. They started at recess and continued at the extended lunch break—by that time, I had had enough and could not maintain my silent battle any longer.

"Do you have head lice again?"

"Who did you beat up this time?"

I could take stupid comments like those, but not the one that hit too close to the fresh wound in my core.

"Did your mom start doing drugs again?"

A couple of the teachers intervened again and pulled me off the other kid ever so gently. I sat in the office for the rest of the day, periodically crying and wailing at the unfairness of it all, while Cory Braxley was interviewed by the vice principal. I received an in-school suspension for fighting, and he got a behavior-reflection sheet for making fun of me, that smug little piece of shit.

I only saw Shelley a handful of times after that. But as with all things in my life, she, too, would leave me, as she was not a counselor for middle schools. With June's end just around the corner, I was soon looking at grade six.

The last day I saw Shelley, she introduced me to the counselor I would be seeing at Lakeview Middle School, Ms. Brenda. She was nice, but I just didn't feel that connection. We had a couple of transition visits so I could get to know her and vice versa before the jump to middle school.

I was glad when the school year was over, though, and I didn't have to see Brenda for a while. She asked the same kind of questions as Shelley, but her tone and voice weren't the same. I thought ahead though, and I figured if I played the game, answered the questions and all that crap, I could still go to counseling and get out of class.

I became less and less likable, even by my standards, and that only served to make the kids avoid me even more. In a way I reveled in it, because it made me different from everyone else—even negative attention was better than none.

The summer between grade five and grade six was one of transition for me—both physically and mentally. Destiny and I went to stay at Josephine's house for a week. Connie came to our place to visit, too, when Mom would make it back to Greenleigh to see us.

I also got my period after months of having to listen to all those stupid twats in my class describe how they went to the bathroom in the middle of the night, or whenever, and found blood in their underwear. It made me ill, having to listen to them describe it as if they were recounting a religious experience—it was a simple bodily function for crissake.

I got mine that summer at the local public pool. Having an aversion to peeing in a public pool, unlike many of my peers, I went to the washroom. When I wiped, there was blood on the toilet paper. I was very stoic about the whole thing. That's how I am about most everything now. A wad of toilet paper worked nicely until Destiny and I got home, where I asked Gran for a sanitary pad.

She shook her head and huffed out a breath. "Great," she said sarcastically. "I knew that would happen soon." She shuffled into the bathroom and came out with a huge sanitary napkin.

"Here," she said as she handed it to me. "This is a super one, 'cause of my menopause. I'll go to the store later and get you small ones."

In the bathroom I was wrapping the humongous pad's wings around my underwear when I heard a soft knock at the door.

"You know you can get pregnant now," said Gran.

"Yeah, I know."

"And you know how that happens, right?"

"Yeah, I know."

"So don't do it, then—you understand?"

"Yeah, I do."

That was the extent of our "talk." Gran was never one for conversation.

In terms of attitude, I learned that if you had a badass one, people wouldn't bother you. But I wasn't that kind of person—I didn't have the self-confidence or the balls to pull off something like that, so I chose the disappear-into-the-background option, and with guarded optimism, I hoped for the best.

I sincerely wished that middle school would prove to be a better experience for me, as I couldn't have tolerated another sad and sorry day at Land Street Elementary.

# Chapter 10

If elementary school was a nightmare, middle school is an anxiety-inducing, self-esteem-bashing incubus hatched from hell—wait—worse than hell. It's a place where the bus drops you off so you can be ripped apart piece by miserable piece by your so-called peers. A place you're so excited to go to right after you get out of elementary school, but within a week you're wishing you were back in elementary. A place where everybody talks about everybody behind their back then talks about how they hate two-faced people.

The teachers are there to teach you crap you will most likely never use. They revel in giving you five hours of homework a night and in-school detention for doing something totally harmless.

The popular kids like the same brands, wear the same

clothes, have the same phones, and are there to make you feel absolutely worthless. If you're not a popular, you can't win. For example, a person can like the same music as a popular and will automatically be called a poser, but when you don't like the same stuff as the populars, you're called a geek/nerd/loser—WTF is up with that?

You're just starting to go through puberty, so your face is covered in red, angry pimples, and the people who haven't gone through puberty make fun of you for it. The Sacred Cows (that's what I called the popular girls) wear padded bras that turn them into double-Cs when they're only an A-cup, and everybody hates everybody else and cuts themselves or has body image issues and is bulimic. And everybody fakes Starbucks obsessions when really they can't stand the stuff.

I spent my first year at Lakeview Middle School trying to be invisible, but was ultimately unsuccessful. I wallowed in my cloud of Darkness, trying to fade into the shadows. At first, no one from my elementary school gave me so much as a "Hi, Freak, you look like hell today." And I certainly didn't speak to any of them, as they were already well established in their respective cliques. The kids from all the other feeder schools were, too.

I did remember my anger management strategies that Shelley had taught me. I practiced them religiously, though I did show my anger in ways that, now that I look back, were bizarre. I didn't shower regularly or wash my hair. My clothes were usually scruffy and old—and in truth, I liked it that way. I was content to flounder amongst the multitude of new faces in the hall. Maybe I could stay unnoticed for my entire three years at Lakeview. But, of course, that was not to be, as my skin was starting to break out, my hair was constantly greasy, and my clothes were from Value Village. Now don't get me wrong, some girls can really do vintage up well in Value Village attire, but I was never one of them. I stood out like a turd in a punch bowl due to my appearance. And that's just a tiny window into my three years of middle school.

My gran practically stopped doing all things that a parent would normally do for a kid. She said she had her hands full enough with having to keep tabs on my mom's current crisis and looking after Des, and that I was old enough to do things for myself. And I still missed Connie terribly—we only saw her once a month now if we were lucky. She was busy with her riding lessons, gymnastics, piano, and God-knows-what-else. I'd talk to her on the phone, though. I'd complain about my horrible days, and she would tell me that I had to try to make friends. Having friends meant I had allies.

The days came and went, fall, winter, spring, and summer. In that year, Momma turned a corner. The way I see it, when you take drugs for a long time and it looks like you either have to stop or you'll die, or alternatively, you know you'll never kick it so you just go at full throttle and hope that the end is quick. Well, I pretty much think she chose the latter. As I watched her spiraling down, my moods sank with her and things got really bad again. The Darkness wrapped itself around me like a heavy shroud, eating away at what little happiness I had. I hated school but at least it was a distraction; home was hell because it gave me too much time to think.

But in all that hell, in the winter of grade seven, I *did* find a couple of friends—they were just as screwed up and lonely as I was.

Norma would wear long-sleeved shirts in the stifling heat, and everyone knew that she cut herself, but she denied it vehemently when people were mean enough to bring it up. Her mom and dad were lawyers and were successful—albeit, only in terms of the lawyer part, because if you're a successful parent, your kid isn't inflicting gaping wounds on her arms.

Norma's parents moved into the school catchment area just as part of their hipster-lawyer-urban-renewal lifestyle, latching on to the latest trend of re-gentrification of old houses in the downtown core—this according to Norma—whatever. Anyway, she came from affluent suburbia to inner city Lakeview Middle School, where the "have-nots" outnumbered the "haves" five to one—what a culture shock!

And then, there is Ishaan—kindhearted, sweet Ishaan. He has been the victim of hounding from both his father and schoolmates for most of his young life. Ishaan is gay, but unfortunately for him, our school population and, more importantly, his father have not progressed enough to be able to accept someone who is not like the majority of our middle school male jock, nerd, or emo population.

Norma's parents were always working, and she lacked any kind of direction from them—except when they occasionally interacted with her to critique her defiant attitude, sullen behavior, and school marks. Ishaan had only his dad, who was a stressed-out dry-cleaning store franchisee trying to make a living supporting Ishaan and his two older sisters, who were both in university. His mother died shortly after she gave birth to him, from complications due to a stroke.

I met Norma in January of grade seven.

• • •

I'm in one of the study carrels in the school library, hiding from the rest of the student body. I hear someone say hi, but it can't possibly be directed at me, so I keep reading my graphic novel and take another bite of my sandwich.

"Hi." I look up, wondering who else would be in the library at lunch—usually it is only me and a few teachers, who try their hardest to ignore me. I turn my head and there stands a girl in a floppy maroon sweater and leggings. Her brown hair is styled so that her bangs fall over her eyes, which are hazel gray and almost the color of smoke.

"Hi?" I respond in a suspicious tone. My eyes do a quick sweep around to see who else is there, in case this is a prank.

"You're in my English class, right?"

"I don't know." I genuinely don't, because I sit at the back, always enter through the rear door, and the only view I get is of the back of people's heads.

"Yeah, you are. I'm Norma. Do you have yesterday's notes? I was absent and so was my other friend in that class. I skipped out, kind of."

"How do you 'kind of' skip out—you either do or you don't—and how do you skip out in middle school?" I was intrigued by this concept. Most days I could manage school, but sometimes I begged Gran to let me stay home if I was having a really bad Dark spell. She always sent me to school, even if I had a fever and was coughing up a lung. "Didn't they call your parents once they realized you weren't there?"

Norma tilts her head, looking mildly inconvenienced at having to explain herself. "Actually, I just stayed home all day—I faked that I was sick. My parents are too busy to argue with me, so they just call the school and clear me. Now, do you have yesterday's notes?"

"You fake sick but you want notes so you can catch up?" To me that sounds contradictory.

"That's my parents' condition—they clear me but insist that I keep up—I'll just photocopy them tonight and bring them back."

Still suspicious, I reach for my English binder, which is tucked away in the corner of the study carrel. "I don't take notes, but you can have the handout we got." I extract it from the mess of papers sticking out of my binder.

"I'll return it tomorrow." Her voice has a flat quality, like she's bored with me already.

"Whatever," I say. "It's not like I'll ever look at it again." I go back to my book.

I have no further contact with Norma, until I meet Ishaan.

About a month later, I'm having a particularly bad day. I had set my alarm clock the night before, but as usual I had trouble sleeping and I slept right through it. Gran is working most mornings, so Des and I can't rely on her. I just grab whatever is on the floor of my room, almost stepping in the cat litter, and rush Des out the door. I go to school looking like a disheveled mess, with a perpetual hair tangle at the back of my head that I try to smooth over but never quite manage to unsnarl.

"Oh—my—God," I hear one of the girls say as I board the bus and walk to the back. Someone giggles. Others pretend to ignore me until I walk past them, and then they snicker and whisper. Everyone avoids eye contact with me, even the losers, who are still a rung or two above me on the social hierarchy. I'm pretty much on my own—the lowest freak on the freak totem pole.

I get to school, go to my locker, endure more stares and giggles, then go to my first class. Again, the looks, snickers, and comments. Why won't they just leave me alone? Skulking to my seat at the back of the class, I open my book to a blank page and cast my eyes down to wait for the teacher.

"Oh my God," murmurs one of the Sacred Cows to her posse, just loud enough so I can hear. "When's the last time you think she washed her hair?" A wave of laughter ripples across the room.

"I dunno," says a kid I call Ass Kisser because of how he sucks up to our English teacher, Ms. Emerson. "Maybe sometime last year." More laughter. Tears well up in my eyes while thousands of previous humiliations cross my mind. He laughs at his joke, and I put my head down. Still I say nothing because if I do, I will lose control and I know I'll hurt him. That's when I hear a shrill voice pierce the laughter.

"Shut up!" The voice is familiar. "Leave her alone." The laughter stops, though only for a moment, clearly out of shock that someone's speaking out. Then the jeers start, not from everyone, just from Sacred Cow, her drones, and Ass Kisser.

"Oh, look—the cutter's standing up for Pig-Pen over there!" says Ass Kisser.

"Who do you think you are, Asshole?" A guy's voice cuts in. I still have my head down so I can't see who it is. "Making people feel like shit! You have no right—just leave her alone."

I begin to feel the tiniest sliver of relief. Who are these people coming to my rescue? Was one of them the girl from the library?

"Oh, now the faggot queer speaks." Ass is angry now.

"That's harassment, you idiot. No one should be subjected to that!" says the boy.

"You know what *you'll* be subjected to later, right? You fucking—"

At that moment, I hear Ms. Emerson's heels enter the class from the hall. "What did you say, Jack?" I look up and see that she has stopped dead in the threshold of the doorway, her brow is furrowed.

"Oh, excuse me, Ms. Emerson. I was talking about a gaming event and it just slipped out." Jack's entire demeanor changes. He is "smooth as silk," as my Gran would say. "Sorry about that, Miss."

Ms. Emerson looks around the classroom, unconvinced. Everyone's eyes dart from me, to Norma, and to the Indian boy sitting across the aisle from her.

"I'd like to speak with you after class." Ms. Emerson's brow arches. "Stay behind, Jack." Jack's face goes plum red. "Okay,

Miss." He smiles at her as she strides in and places her books on the desk, but when she turns to write on the board, he twists to his right and makes a cutting motion across his neck to the Indian guy across from Norma.

Indian Guy then proceeds to flip him off, which I think is ballsy, because Jack the Ass Kisser is almost twice his size.

I can't believe this really happened. Did two people I don't even know defend me?

I keep my eyes downcast, as I don't have the courage to make eye contact with the two kids who spoke up, but after a while I feel that I owe them at least a thank you. I stare at them until they notice, then I mouth, "Thank you." Norma shrugs her shoulders and gives me a half smile. The Indian guy nods in my direction. That's the extent of our exchange that day.

• • •

The Indian guy comes to English class the next day with a fresh bruise on his cheek—it's angry red in the middle and purply-blue at the outsides. I have a horrible feeling that he didn't walk into a door or anything, because Ass Kisser smiles in a most sinister way and asks, "How's your face today, Faggot?"

At lunch, it's all I can do to muster up the courage to venture into the cafeteria and ask him how he got the bruise. If Ass Kisser punished him for daring to defend me, then I had to thank him personally.

"Hi," I say softly. Norma and Indian Guy are sitting at the end of a long table, their heads together, scrolling through their Instagram feeds. They look up at me suspiciously.

"Hi," they reply in unison.

"I want to thank you guys for yesterday."

"No worries," says Norma. "This is Ishaan, by the way."

I smile weakly at him and survey the big purple and blue bruise just under his eye. "Did you get that because of me?" I gesture toward his cheek.

"Maybe…. What if I did?"

I knew it. That bastard Jack the Ass Kisser punched him in the cheek because he defended me. "I'm so sorry. He's such a jerk. Next time just let him talk. I'm used to it anyway."

"No fucking way!" says Ishaan.

"You can't ignore that shit," says Norma angrily. "Ignoring it makes it okay. And what he was saying to you was not okay." She looks at Ishaan, then back at me. "Even if, and please don't take this wrong, even if he kinda has a point. You know, about the clothes and the hair…"

"And the smell," says Ishaan. "Is that cat urine?" He waves his hand in front of his nose.

"I do have a cat."

"Does he have a litter box?"

"In my room."

"Maybe he's using your clothes instead," he says. Norma snorts out a laugh. I smile and, surprisingly, am not offended by what they say.

"Maybe tonight I'll move the cat box outside. And use the washing machine to wash my clothes."

"Capital idea," says Ishaan. "Use the shower, too."

Norma glares at him, then turns to me. "Sit down with

us and stop hermitizing, or whatever you call it, in the library. You look like you could use some friends."

"Yeah, but sit a couple seats away," Ishaan jokes. Norma slaps his arm and I laugh. Our conversation is light—what school did I attend before Lakeview, do I have any siblings, where do I live. I respond and ask the same questions. We come from very different backgrounds—no surprise there. But in an unspoken way, the three of us know that we have one major thing in common—we are outcasts because we are different. I have that feeling I had when I used to talk to Shelley. Like there is hope for me. I feel a small degree of redemption, a sliver of release from the days at school that I spend alone, which I know are very much my own doing.

That night, I have a long shower and throw a couple of loads of laundry in the washer, along with some of Des's stuff.

Gran looks up from her laptop keno game long enough to see me toting the laundry hamper back to my room. "What in the world? You feeling all right?" Her tone is dry and sarcastic.

"Yeah, no thanks to you," I mumble under my breath as I skulk up the stairs.

I did feel all right—I felt a little better because, for the first time in middle school, possibly for the first time in my school career since grade two, I could say that I had made friends.

# Chapter 11

Next day, *I* had friends to sit with in the cafeteria. In order to prove that they had come to the defense of a deserving human being, I had showered, washed and combed my hair, and put on my freshly laundered jeans and sweatshirt. People did double takes on the bus, but thankfully didn't comment beyond a roll of the eye and whispers.

...

My shoulders are back, my eyes are focused straight ahead, not at the floor, as I walk into English class that morning. If I deserve Norma's and Ishaan's support, maybe I'm not a total piece of wasted space after all.

I sit upright at my desk, not making eye contact with any of the students who are already there. A few seconds later, Ishaan and Norma enter, look at me, and smile. I smile back, able to breathe again. But the relief doesn't last long. Soon Jack strolls in; his face sports a mix of disdain and disgust clearly aimed at Ishaan. He swaggers toward his desk, but not before intentionally shoving himself against Ishaan's shoulder and bumping his books against Norma.

"Watch what you're doing!" Norma calls out.

"Oh! Sorry. I didn't realize my own strength." Jack snickers at his own lame comment. "Hey, you." He motions to me with his head. "Why aren't you sitting up here with your freaky friends?" Some of the kids laugh, but not as many as yesterday. I feel a little hopeful that Jack may be losing some of his audience, yet I'm angry that I'm subjected to constant ridicule because I don't fit their idea of acceptable or normal or fashionable…or clean.

I sit still as stone, rage boiling inside me, rising up to the back of my throat again. My breathing deepens and my face flushes red as I cradle my pen in my hand. It only takes a split second for my mood to change, but everyone has a boiling point—and Ass Kisser has pushed all my buttons. My hands itch to grab his neck and snap it. My teeth clench, then I can't keep it in anymore, so I just let it out.

"Why don't you just shut your fucking shit-filled mouth and leave everyone alone, Jack—you ass-kissing piece of crap?" I feel light-headed after I finish the last word—*crap;* euphoric from letting off toxic steam that has built up over the last few months. Some of the kids gasp. I think it's because this may be the first time they've heard my voice.

"Who said that?" I hear someone say. "Did she say that?" A swell of laughter spreads across the room.

"What did you say?" Jack squints at me as he furrows his brows.

"She said shut up and leave people alone." That's Norma. Jack whirls around to face her.

"Ass kisser." That is Ishaan. More laughter, after which Jack's at a loss for words, probably for the first time in his life. He's had the wind knocked out of his sails. I feel victorious.

I want so much to have the courage to do this every day, to shut down all the bullies who make me feel subhuman. At this moment, in this room, it is the perfect storm. A precise mix of anger, audacity, and the new desire to reciprocate an act of kindness have enabled me speak out against someone who has no idea how words can cut through someone's very soul. I may never get the nerve to do it again, but today works in my favor, because Jack just shakes his head, whispers a profanity under his breath, and sits down hard in his chair, legs sprawled out in front to convey his contempt at having been cut down.

Then in walks Ms. Emerson, all distracted and shuffling some reports that are to be handed back today, and she very nearly trips over Jack's feet. "Can you please sit up straight!" Ms. Emerson's voice is shrill. "I just about fell and broke my neck." Muted laughter rises and falls.

This was really not Jack's day.

• • •

I join Norma and Ishaan at their table for lunch, and though I'm not much of a conversationalist, I try my hardest to impress them. It's a little awkward, as Norma is staring at her phone and Ishaan is reading a book.

Finally Norma comes up for air and gazes at me as she lays her phone down. "So what are you doing this weekend?" she asks.

I shrug. "Not much." There's a pause in conversation, then Ishaan looks up from his book.

"Did you know that thousands of letters are sent to God every year by way of Jerusalem?" He points at the page he's reading. "It says here that the Jerusalem post office takes the letters very seriously, and has—get this—a Letters to God department! The staff sends them to a rabbi, who slides them into the cracks of the Western Wall, whatever that is, where they join the million or so messages per year that are delivered in person. You can also fax or e-mail messages, and they'll print them out and put them in that wall, too."

"Isn't God supposed to just hear you, wherever you are?" I ask.

"Or," continues Ishaan, "you can snail mail it—the address is 'God, Jerusalem.'" He looks flabbergasted by this fact. Norma smiles and shakes her head. Then there is an awkward silence.

"Do you believe in God?" she asks.

I shrug. "I believe in something." I chew on the side of my mouth. "I call her the Ultimate Being."

Norma nods. "Cool." More awkward silence.

"Do you really cut yourself?" I blurt. Norma's eyes widen.

"Whoa—that's kind of private." She pulls her sleeves even farther down over her hands.

"Norma isn't ready to share everything with you yet, obviously," Ishaan cautions. I mentally note that I have to practice my social skills.

Norma checks over her shoulders, then she leans across the table and speaks softly. "I got some weed from my cousin—she gave me a joint. You wanna get together this weekend? We can go behind the school and smoke it." Ishaan and I look at each other, unsure how to respond.

"I dunno," I say, raising a brow. I glance over my shoulder, too. "I mean, don't they tell us not to smoke that? It's dangerous and still illegal, isn't it?" I look to Ishaan for confirmation.

"It is." He closes his book with a snap.

Norma purses her lips. "Whatever. Are you in or not?" she asks impatiently. I wait for Ishaan to answer. If he says yes, I won't say no.

"Okay, I guess I'll try it, but I've never even smoked cigarettes. I'll probably die if I inhale," he declares.

"Well, you have to inhale, or you won't get high," Norma whispers. "I don't want to talk about it anymore—too many ears around here."

We didn't talk about it again until Friday after school. We decided to meet at Ishaan's house, because he was closest to Lakeview. We were going to hide behind one of the portables and try to figure out how to smoke the joint without puking.

"I'm not sure we should be doing this," I say as we walk toward the school parking lot. I keep thinking of all the stuff they told us in school about smoking weed—how it can make you depressed and can cause psychosis. And then I think about all the adults I know who are nuts and screwed up and never smoked a joint in their life. I'm torn between images of my mother's substance abuse and the need to prove my friendship to Norma and Ishaan.

"I'm absolutely sure we *shouldn't* be doing this," quips Ishaan.

"Oh, *please*," hisses Norma. "Three-quarters of the school population has done this already."

We find an acceptable spot at a portable, close to the stairs. At least if we faint, we'll have somewhere to sit, instead of falling onto gravel.

Norma reaches into her satchel and pulls out the joint and a pack of matches. She puts the open end between her lips and strikes a match—it doesn't catch, so she tries another. It works. As Ishaan and I watch, she brings the joint to her lips and inhales. I'm fairly certain that she's never smoked before, as she expels the smoke with a deep, throaty cough. When the coughing fit subsides, she takes another drag, this time smaller, and manages to keep the smoke down.

Ishaan tries next. He inhales, coughs, chokes, and passes it to me, not even daring a second drag. I decide I should turn out the best effort and impress my friends, so I take a shallow drag and inhale. Of course I cough it out, but I try again, and this time I hold it down. I pass it on to Norma. Inhale, pass, repeat, until the joint is a tiny ember, which we let float to the ground. I feel my foot move to stomp it out. I actually didn't will my foot to move—it kind of just did it of its own accord. That freaks me out a little. I remember thinking that time is going by a lot slower—but I can't remember what I'm saying and can't finish my sentences.

Looking back through my foggy islands of recollection, the next few highs were better. I felt floaty. Music sounded incredible while high, and it got hard to hold back laughter. Time slowed down or sometimes sped up. Food tasted incredible, and I usually got very hungry, plus if I was outside, I noticed that things looked different, like the treetops, the ground. I could see another side or another angle of the world. If I was inside, I might become fascinated by everyday things like posters or the patterns on wallpaper. Sometimes I could actually "hear" myself thinking much more intensely than normal.

It didn't happen all that often at that time, but when it did, all that made us feel like we could take on anything. Thirteen-year-olds trying to act like we knew what we were doing and didn't care how much it hurt us. The good feeling was only temporary, and the same old feeling always came back after the high was gone, sometimes even worse. After the highs came the punishing lows.

By the end of the school year, we were inseparable.

# Chapter 12

Like I said, my mom reached a point in her addiction where she had to either stop or run headfirst into a wall. Momma not only ran into a wall, she lunged at it—and in the end, the wall won. That summer, we got a call from Toronto General that Mom was in intensive care with acute septicemia. Gran had no idea what that was, so Destiny and I checked online, and it wasn't good.

They told us that Mom got septicemia from dirty needles and that she was brought in too late to help her. Her organs were already shutting down. Mom and her dealer boyfriend were too wasted to realize she was sick. Barely coherent and slipping in and out of consciousness, she died from complications arising out of the infection. We stayed with her the whole time; Gran wouldn't let Mom's boyfriend near her.

I didn't—and I still don't—like to talk much about the entire ordeal. Truth is, I was angry. As much as I loved Momma, I didn't cry at her funeral. My anger took up too much space for me to feel much of anything besides rage: rage for losing my mother to drug abuse years before she died: rage at my Gran for not keeping Momma home. I even felt rage during the wake. Our town house living room was crowded with people talking and eating, introducing themselves like it was a church social or something, and my mother was dead.

"Jesus—it sounds like a fucking party in here. I can't stand it," I hiss to Des and Connie.

Des nods. "Do you know that, in some cultures, they have literal parties after a funeral? Like the ancient Celts or modern Ghanaians."

Connie rolls her eyes. "Really, Des?"

"What? It's true."

"You guys are just as bad." I walk away and join Ishaan and Norma, who are huddled awkwardly in a corner. My sisters aren't angry or horribly upset at all, it seems.

I grew up idolizing a person I barely even knew, unable to figure out why I felt that unconditional loyalty. Connie and Des were sad, of course, but afterward, they were so much more easily distracted that I felt I was the only one mourning my mother.

Of course, in addition to deep sadness and anger, what I feared most became my new reality. After the funeral, the Darkness and empty feeling came back stronger, taking me down like quicksand. So I buried it. I buried it deep inside me and never let it out, because if I did, I'd be afraid of what would happen. I buried it with attitude and recklessness, carelessness and contempt. I built a wall around me—only then did I know I'd survive.

The people that kept me from sinking to the bottom and suffocating were Destiny, Norma, and Ishaan. I stuck with the people who were there for me when I was my most apathetic. If it wasn't for them, I don't think I could have come out of that deep mass that was pushing me down and pressing the light out of my soul.

"You never know how strong you are until being strong is your only choice." Bob Marley said that.

All the crap that life threw at us was a little easier to take because of Norma and Ishaan. They gave me licence to be reckless. It was a welcome distraction—one that I craved.

Fast forward to November of grade eight.

• • •

"Hey, wut up?" Ishaan slams his books down on the greasy cafeteria table next to Norma and me. "What we can do this weekend?" he asks.

"I'm really not down for doing anything lame again. Weed just makes me paranoid and I don't have any money." I scrunch up the plastic wrap from my sandwich and toss it to the bin, missing it. "Jeez, now I gotta go pick that up." I walk by the Sacred Cows, and hear a definite "Oh my God" and giggles as I pick up the wrapping and toss it in the trash.

"Go fuck yourselves," is my cool response. Being crude

freaks them out. *Can't stand you—die and go to hell.* As I turn to swagger back to our table, I see that Ishaan and Norma are deep in conversation. I catch the last bit of the discussion as I sit down.

"So if you take those two together, you get really messed up."

"Take what?" I say.

"If you take Ambien and then drink vodka or some other shit, you get really messed up—I was doing some research and found it on a totally effed-up site last night." Norma sounds excited.

"How did we get from 'what are we doing this weekend' to mixing Ambien and vodka?" I ask.

"Norma was just making a suggestion," remarks Ishaan. "You were the one who brought up drugs."

"The hell I did; I said I didn't have the money to buy weed and it makes me paranoid anyway."

"Well, this is free." Norma's smile is saccharine. "My mother, Ms. Huge-Ass Lawyer, needs Ambien to sleep, 'cause money flies out of her asshole continuously and that keeps her up at night." Ishaan and I giggle at the visual.

I screw up my face. "I have trouble sleeping and I don't have money flying out of my hinny."

Ish rolls his eyes and looks over his shoulder. "We were saying that if you take Ambien and drink after you take it, you get high."

"Really?"

"Yeah, really."

"They post this stuff on the Internet?"

"That's not the point—the point is that we got our weekend." Ish's voice cracks with excitement. "*If* Norma gets the Ambien—how many can you get?"

"I don't want her to suspect—three maybe…six at the most."

"Are they prescription?"

"Duh. That's why I can't take that many. *And* why we need alcohol—to 'enhance' the effects." She uses air quotes when she says *enhance*. There's a tingling in my stomach. A mix of excitement and apprehension. I know drugs are trouble—my mother's death is proof of that. I'm confronted with the decision to do the right thing or do something stupid. Should I heed that vision of my mother lying decimated in a hospital bed due to drug abuse, or should I listen to the voice that pulls me down into the stupidity abyss where you do dumb things to be cool, to go along with friends, and to be able to brag about it.

Naturally, the stupid voice wins out. "I'm in," I say softly.

"As am I," echoes Ishaan.

"So, where are we gonna do this?" I look from Ishaan to Norma.

"My house, of course," Norma replies. "My dad has enough vodka to kill a horse. He'll never know it's missing. He goes through it so quickly that for him, it's like opening a bottle of Perrier." She smiles. "They're going out tonight. If you guys get permission, you can sleep over."

It was a plan.

Ishaan begged his father to let him sleep over, and with a

little egging on from his sister, his dad relented. I felt sorry for him—his father couldn't get beyond his son's sexuality. Ishaan was the only son and he was gay. And then there was me. I don't think Gran would have cared if I had grown a horn and spewed beer out of my mouth—all I had to do was *tell* Gran where I was going. She didn't mind not having me around, so I figured I was doing her a favor.

• • •

That evening, I stuff some extra sweats, a toothbrush, and socks into my backpack. I walk to Ishaan's house and wait outside. Not thirty seconds later, his door opens and there he is, backpack over his shoulders.

"Hey," Ish says with a little wave. Gracefully, he descends his front steps to join me—I wish I had his poise and natural refinement.

As we walk, I want to ask the question, but in the same instant, I don't want to sound like I'm sucking out. "Are you ready to do this?"

"Hell, yeah—can't wait." Though his words are bold, he sounds less than convinced. "You?"

"Me too," I lie. We're both quiet.

"Even, like, after what happened to your mom? You're not freaking out?"

I shrug. "What do you think it'll feel like?" I ask.

"I dunno. Probably we're gonna feel really good. At least, I hope so. I hope we don't, like, freak out or something, or die." He laughs nervously and takes out his phone. "Norma just texted me; her parents left and she's got the pills and the vodka." He puts his phone back in his pocket.

"I hope that we don't end up like one of these celebrities, dead in a bathtub or something like that." My lips are dry and my stomach is tingling again.

"Come on, you know we're not that screwed up—even for being screwed up." That makes me laugh.

When we get to Norma's, we knock politely and then let ourselves in. "Hey, Norma, it's us," Ish says.

"Hey!" Norma comes bounding up the stairs to meet us. "Oh my God, you scared the crap out of me; I thought my parents came back." She huffs out a big breath. "Didn't anyone ever tell you to wait until someone answers the door?" The music from the basement resounds throughout the house.

"Sorry," drawls Ishaan. "The door was open."

"Yeah, we thought you were expecting us," I remark.

"Yeah—no, I'm sorry—just kinda jumpy." She scratches her head nervously. "So what do you guys think? They'll be gone awhile, but they'll be back. Do you wanna start?"

Our eyes dart from one to the other in a kind of eye dance, then finally Norma speaks. "Okay, you scaredy-shits, I'll go first." She turns on her heel and heads downstairs to the game room, her short hair bouncing as she skips. Ishaan and I follow her sheepishly into the laundry room. She opens a cupboard and pulls out a water bottle filled to the top, three Styrofoam cups, and a plastic bag with three little pills.

"I could only get three. She didn't have that many left." She uncaps the water bottle and pours the liquid evenly into the cups. She hands one to me and the other to Ish. "I researched that you should drink the alcohol first, then find a spot to lie down and take the pills, 'cause they might fuck you up."

"You researched this?" Ish says.

Norma raises her brows. "Are you gonna do this or are you just gonna make fun?"

"She's right," I say quietly. "We should be ready for anything. And we should have a pail, too, in case we feel like we have to puke."

Ish angles his head toward me. "I think if we're at the point that we're puking, we won't have the presence of mind to do so in a pail so we can spare the broadloom."

Norma laughs. "Okay, enough—come on, let's just do this." She holds up her glass and takes a big swig of her vodka, followed by a wince and a bout of coughing. "Oh God, that's awful! How the hell does he drink this shit?"

Ishaan and I follow suit and have much the same reaction.

We sip the rest of the vodka as we sit on the plush couches. I start to feel a distinct buzz almost instantly, and the feeling only grows as we force down the rest.

"When do we take the Ambien?" My vision isn't keeping up with my head as I move to look at Norma.

"I guess now…I guess." She laughs out loud, which makes us laugh like crazy.

"Are you guessing, now is good, do you guess?" Ish slurs.

She plucks out a little pill from the plastic bag and then reaches over so we can each take one. Ish takes his, and then I try to claw one out. Being very clumsy at this point, I drop it somewhere on the rug.

"Oh shit. Get another one, Norma—I lost it." My speech is slurred, too.

"Uh—no, I can't." Norma settles into the couch like she's cradled into a cocoon. "I'm too drunk to move, and in a minute or so, I'll be too high to function."

"That sucks, Faith. That really sucks. Look for…" Ishaan's words trail into obscurity.

He is feeling pretty good, too—even in my drunken state, I can tell.

He didn't say another word after that. I don't know how long I watched them both, but they sat very still and just stared into the distance, their eyes glazed over. I felt sorry for myself for losing my little pill so I couldn't get high. Then I just let the music wash over me.

I dozed off awhile later, but was awakened by Norma's mother screaming at the top of her lungs. It seems that mixing Ambien and vodka makes you do weird stuff. Ishaan was found asleep in the bathtub with hydrogen peroxide in his hair. Apparently, you can't leave it in that long, because his hair was pumpkin orange for months.

We got into a lot of trouble. Norma's mom had no idea we took her Ambien. It was the rest of the vodka in the water bottle that tipped her off. She called Gran and Ishaan's dad and ratted us out. We weren't allowed to go over there anymore. Norma and Ishaan were totally grounded, except, of course, for going to school. Gran just yelled and threw stuff at me, but grounding me was too much effort. That would mean that she'd actually have to put some energy into being my guardian.

I also got a call from Connie the next day, and, shit, did she have a thing or two to say about the entire sorry-ass incident.

"What the hell did you think you were doing? You're in grade eight, for God's sake, Faith. Gran told me you guys were passed-out drunk at that kid's house."

"Oh, hi, Connie. I'm fine, thanks, and how are you?" My tone is business-like. "Yes, it has been a long time since we spoke. So sorry we haven't kept in touch, but apparently your shit doesn't stink and you're too good for me now."

I hear a long exhale, followed by a pause. "Okay, you're pissed at me 'cause I haven't been down there, right?"

"Do you think I care if I haven't seen you in months?"

Another pause. "Faith, stop making this about me—I called because Gran doesn't know what to do anymore. She says those losers you hang out with are a bad influence on you."

I laugh out loud at my grandmother's analysis of what constitutes a bad influence on children. "Connie, are you for real right now? Like, do you hear yourself!" I can't help it, I am shouting. "Our mother is dead, Gran doesn't care if we live or die, you left us to go live in Disney World with your rich father's family, and I'm stuck here playing 'mom' to our younger sister!" I take in a deep breath. "Yeah, you're right, Connie—it's all Ishaan and Norma's fault. I'm not a product of my environment at all—there are no drug dealers around here, making buying shit as easy as going to the corner store, and my middle school is a preppy college, like the one you go—"

"Okay, shut up!" Connie yelps. "First, that's not true about Gran at all; she does care. And nobody *made* you drink—you chose to. Don't give me that 'poor me' thing, 'cause that's Mom talking right there, so fucking woman up! Second, I'm busy studying because I want to get into a decent university. Studying is when you open a book or look over your notes before a test—try it sometime! And third, I know you guys took something else with that vodka. Don't bullshit me, 'cause I know you did! You don't color your own hair, like your friend did, if you're passed out on vodka alone!" I feel my face get hot. Did she figure it out? And if she did, did she tell Gran—or, worse, Josie?

"Now, I'm going to repeat the question, Faith. What the hell do you think you're doing?"

"Okay." I let out a heavy sigh. "I screwed up. I'm sorry—it was a stupid thing to do."

"That's putting it mildly. A stupid thing to do would be forgetting to put on a helmet when you're riding your bike. This is completely off-the-charts stupid!"

"Okay, I know. It was irresponsible and dangerous."

"You took Ambien or something with the vodka, right?"

I pause. Then finally I answer, "Not me, but they did. I lost mine."

"Shit! I knew it," she hisses at me. "You're friggin' lucky you didn't die, you stupid—"

"Okay, Connie. I said I'm sorry—jeez. I told you, I'm done with that stuff." I hear breathing on the other end.

"All right. But I swear to God, if you ever—"

"I won't! I promise." The floor creaks upstairs. Gran is working, so Destiny is probably on her way down from doing her homework.

"Are you coming over this weekend?" I ask, forever hopeful. "Destiny misses you, too."

"Not sure," she answers curtly. "I'll have to see."

I don't respond, as I feel her reply merits none. "So, anything else, then?" I ask.

"I guess not," she replies. "Stay outta trouble—I'll call again."

"Fine." I want to add *bitch*, but think better of it because I remember how much I hate that word.

"Say hi to Des for me, and remember, she looks up to you. That should be reason enough for you not to screw up again. We'll talk soon." Then the line clicks dead.

I feel a tap on my shoulder and I jump. "Jesus, Des, you startled me."

"Who was that?" she asks as she heads toward the kitchen.

"No one. Someone doing a survey," I lie. I am getting really good at it.

"Oh." She opens the fridge.

"So did you finish your homework?" I ask.

"Almost—I did my math, now I just have to finish up my science, then I'm done." My little sister, Destiny. Now there is a kid who loves school, despite all the odds stacked against her. She's smart, but not the kind of smart that you have to work at; she's the kind of smart that comes from common sense. She can apply anything she learns to a new situation—a real think-outside-the-box kind of smart. One day, she could really make something of herself, do some good, like be a doctor and cure cancer, or go to Mars, or something like that. Then there's me—I can't even figure out integers. I think about what Connie said.

"Maybe I'll go up and do some of my math, too." What the hell—it won't kill me to try. I didn't bring home my books, but I still have a textbook that I thought I lost under my bed.

Destiny looks up from her peanut butter sandwich with wide eyes. "Really? You're gonna do your homework?" She knows me too well. "That's great, Faith. Wow!"

*Jesus! It's pretty sad when your little sister sounds like your kindergarten teacher.*

"Yup! Here I go—wish me luck."

"Good luck." She smiles at me and chomps on her sandwich.

I did do my homework that night—it's amazing what the brain retains, though I hardly listen during class as my attention is constantly drifting. I struggled, but I went back a few lessons and, hey, I got it. After that, I thought again about what Connie said; about setting an example for Destiny. Connie has balls even bringing that up, knowing full well that she has pretty much washed her hands of any responsibility toward us. I think about it a lot. There's no point in dragging Destiny into my bitter little world, but if Connie thinks she can tell me what to do, she's crazy.

I hate to say it, but Ishaan, Norma, and I didn't learn our lesson either. I mean, if you're going to go ahead and ignore every lesson that's been taught to you about drug and alcohol abuse, do you really think we'd learn something from our own experiences and not do it again?

We were rebels and badasses. We were certain that acting out against our parents and every other adult who controlled us would be payback for all the screwed-up things they did to us. In our hearts we knew that it would hurt them; we wanted it to hurt. But in the process of hurting them, we were hurting ourselves a thousand times more.

# Chapter 13

Grade nine came with lightning speed in a dense fog of weed-induced stupors, having spent the summer of my fifteenth year mostly high on Norma's little bags of tricks. September rolled in, and so did my first year at Centennial Secondary School, to which I said, "A-goddamn-men to that." In terms of my personal appearance, just as a point of reference and to enhance visuals, I had graduated from looking like I was wearing Cinderella's hand-me-downs to wearing Value Village clothing like I meant it—with a slightly gritty edge and a hint of sexualized adolescent.

Norma helped me out in the fashion department, as she had a real flair for vintage—in fact, I'll go as far as to say that I almost felt attractive. And for what it's worth, Connie did try to call more often and come over more regularly, which

I hastily attributed to guilt. I often reminded her about *her* equal responsibility to set an example for her little sisters, and I heartily stressed the plural *s* in *sisters*.

We started out high school exactly as we expected. Norma, Ish, and I were all in different homerooms. The administrators thought that somehow separating us would prevent us from hanging out with each other—duh. Plan did not work.

We found lots of ways to chill together, mostly in the cafeteria during breaks and then in the evenings. And since no one could stop us, we were allowed to hang out again, with some provisos, of course. No drinking, no drugs, no weed. We had managed to convince our parents that our immature judgment had led us to test our boundaries—and make horrible mistakes. But now we knew our limitations and wouldn't take advantage and we were so sorry and blah, blah, blah, blah, blah.

It was all bullshit, of course. What's amazing is that our parents/guardians fell for it over and over. Oh hell, you can't blame them; they must have hope. Otherwise they'd have to admit to themselves that they're crappy role models and raised us wrong.

By the time November rolled around, I had one hell of an attitude. I dressed mostly in black, to match my disposition, with my belly exposed and my boobs in a bra that made them look like bullets. I had grown to be an unlovable young person. It was easier to be pissed off at everyone—it helped me deal with the Darkness if I was angry all the time.

Gran was always on my back about some stupid thing: pick up your clothes, clean your room, make your lunch, do your homework (which I did in secret, just to piss her off).

Christmas was staring us down, and in a few weeks we would be on holiday. Since we were an "equal-opportunity school," some of the staff members, who felt particularly generous with their time, offered to take the grade nines snow tubing before the break. The teachers kept going on and on about our behavior and their expectations, and, of course, we were all angelic and everything and swore up and down that we would behave. We even signed a contract, which was attached to our permission slip letters and requests for payment. By the way, I never had to pay for trips, because of my "family situation." Sometimes that embarrassed me to hell, but it was either that or I didn't get to go.

Anyway, Norma, Ish, and I were freaking out at the idea. What better way to enjoy a great high than to go shooting a bazillion miles an hour down the side of Blue Mountain totally buzzed out of your head? So yeah, we were in.

Since it was an overnighter, we all packed a duffel bag, which they checked for inappropriate substances—like we would be stupid enough to put it in our suitcases.

Connie, who had kept in touch after sermonizing over the Ambien incident, made a pre-emptive call the night before we left for Blue Mountain.

"Hey."

I'll admit, it always cheers my perpetually gloomy mood when I pick up the phone and hear her voice. "Hi, Connie. What's up?"

"What's up with you?" she says. "Blue Mountain tomorrow?"

"Yeah," I answer. "It's kinda lame, but what the hell." I'm trying to be cool.

"It's not lame; you'll have a lot of fun. I went there with my school a couple years ago. Just keep an open mind."

"Okay, I will. Hey, you know…" I pause, feeling awkward and a bit like a brownnoser. "I'm trying to do my homework more."

"That's awesome—so proud of you."

It's surprising how six little words can lift a person's state of mind. "Thanks."

"Lemme talk to Des."

"Okay, she's right here." I go to hand the phone off to Des when I hear Connie shout something out.

"Wait! Before you put Des on, do me a favor."

"Sure—what?"

"No drugs and no drinking on your trip, okay? You don't have to admit you were going to or anything, but just—just not there. See it for what it is. I want to hear what you think of it all."

"Think of what?"

"You'll know what I'm talking about when you see it. Promise, okay?"

"You're so weird. Here's Des." I don't promise her anything, but before I hand the phone over, I think about the progress we've made and how nice she's being to me, so my icy attitude melts a little. "I'll try."

• • •

"Hi, guys," chirps the enthusiastic hotel rep, smiling from ear to ear. I mistrust people who are overly happy or enthusiastic. "Welcome to Blue Mountain. You're going to have a great time, but before we can start the fantastic activities we have planned for you, we need to get you into your rooms. Follow me to the front desk, and we'll get you all settled in." The ninety or so of us tromp through the snow as she leads us from the school bus into the hotel. Norma, Ishaan, and I are at the very rear.

"So what do you think we're going to do today?" I ask.

"Uh, maybe go snow tubing?" Ish's bone-dry responses are always at the ready.

"I know that—I mean, after that stuff."

"I hope we get some time to enjoy nature—go out for a walk or something later on tonight." A corner of Norma's mouth curls into a smile.

"Yeah, later on tonight," Ish murmurs. "Maybe we can partake of some of that combustible herbage you have hidden in your bra." I smile at Ish. He can make anything sound classy.

We split up and go to our assigned rooms, agreeing to find a way to duck out for a smoke.

Norma and I are assigned to bunk with two other girls who couldn't come up with another pair to sleep with—a girl who has just immigrated from Portugal and doesn't speak any English and a girl named Shawna who still picks her nose and eats it. Brilliant.

Ishaan has to bunk with a trio of techie geeks who spend their evenings and weekends speaking Klingon and who don't have enough other geeks to make up a foursome. Even more brilliant.

• • •

I admit it: Snow tubing was actually fun. But I can't let anyone know that. Only the total losers let on that they were enjoying themselves. Even the teachers had fun, for crissake. We all came out of the experience with rosy cheeks, no broken bones, and hungrier than we'd been in a hell of a long time.

After changing out of our wet clothes and heavy boots into attire appropriate for dinner, we all reconvene in the hotel restaurant. We get to sit where we want, so, of course, I sit with Ishaan and Norma and wolf down dinner like I've never seen food.

"When do you think we can get outside?" Ishaan asks, not shifting his gaze from his plate.

"We're going to have to play that one by ear," Norma answers, her mouth full of portobello mushroom burger.

"I think maybe we'll have to try to go for a walk before bedtime," I offer. "The information letter said they were going to have supervisors posted in our halls for the night." We speak in hushed voices so the losers sitting with us at dinner won't hear and rat us out.

"I'm glad somebody read it. Shit, they think of everything," cusses Norma. We sit silently for a few minutes, thinking.

"Can we just ask if we can go for a walk to see the stars or something lame like that?" Ish asks.

"Yeah, okay, Ish." Norma rolls her eyes. "And then maybe, if, by a thousand to one, they say yes, we'll end up needing teachers to come with us, and then maybe the entire grade nine population will want to come for a stroll in the moonlight, too."

I sip the last of my water and push the rest of my wings away—and then it comes to me.

"Let's just go," I say. "What are they gonna do if we get caught?"

"They can call our parents and tell them to come get us." Ish feigns annoyance.

"They won't. We'll be back before they know we're gone. You and I will go first, Norma, like we're going to the bathroom. Then, Ish, you come in a few minutes." I make up the plan as I speak. "We can grab our coats upstairs and then leave through the side entrance at the end of our hall. Let's meet in the little clearing at the side of the hotel. Then we can find a spot... maybe in the woods? Won't that be nice—like that song by John Denver...'Rocky Mountain High.'" That just blurted out.

"Wow, you're really thinking tonight." Norma smiles.

"John who?" asks Ish.

My Gran listens to John Denver. He was a seventies country singer who died in a plane crash. I like his stuff but I'd die before admitting to it. "Never mind—just do it," I say. Norma and I get up first.

"Do I ever have to pee," I say loud enough for the others at the table to hear.

"Yeah, me too—like my bladder's gonna burst," echoes Norma.

"Little too much information," says the girl next to me, her mouth twisted to show us how grossed out she is.

"Shut your hole," says Norma. And off we go.

We get to our room, scoop up our coats, and exit through the side door, then we wait for Ishaan. In a few minutes, the side door opens and out walks Ish.

"Okay, let's go," he says, tromping his way toward us. "We need to find a more private spot. Norma, you got a lighter?"

"Duh" is all she says. She sticks her hands in her pockets and begins walking toward the woods. Ishaan catches up to her as I lag behind, quite intentionally.

"Hope we don't get lost in there," he says to no one in particular, his tone betraying some concern.

"I wouldn't worry about that," says Norma. She turns and points to our footprints in the snow. "See?" We don't have to worry about finding our way back, because there is a fresh blanket of snow and our tracks are plainly visible.

They continue to walk ahead a few paces and chatter softly about something or other, but I hang back and just take in the scene around me.

As we walk, I look skyward and catch sight of the moon, high in the sky, surrounded by millions of tiny points of light like a quilted blanket of distant suns. I've never seen a sky so clear, so inky blue against the white contrast of fresh snow on the tall pines that line our path like wintry sentinels. It's so quiet, so majestic.

We find a clearing and stop, our breath making vapor clouds in the crisp night air. For a long moment, our gazes feast on the stately beauty of the Canadian north in all its soundless tranquility. This must be what Connie was talking about. I let it feed my inner peace.

"So do you guys wanna smoke?" asks Norma, fumbling around in her bra and finally producing the joint. "Ah, here it is." She winds and finishes the end, then pulls a lighter out of her pocket. As I look at the splendor around me, I decide that the moment would be tainted if my mind is in any way altered by smoking pot. I look at her and shake my head.

"You never know how strong you are until being strong is your only choice." Bob Marley said that.

"I think I'm gonna pass this time." My gaze is once again drawn to the dots in the sky. I imagine the distance between us and the points of light and think about the fact that some of those suns might have already lived their lives and burned out, but we are only getting the light just now, right this very second. And then I think of the billions of years that the suns have shone brightly in the night sky, and how their light at this very moment was meant for me to see, right here in this exact spot. I feel both very important and insignificantly small.

"Why?" asks Norma, surprised.

"Because I want to just be me—not me on weed—and see this."

"But it's better with weed." She brings the joint to her lips and lights the end expertly, drawing a deep drag into her lungs. She passes it to Ishaan. "The experience is enhanced. It's better, clearer even."

I shake my head again and keep my eyes looking up.

"Maybe I don't want it enhanced. Maybe I want it just the way it is." I wipe my nose on my sleeve and marvel at the Milky Way and the moon on the other side of the snowy mountain in the background. "Is it so bad if we just look at the sky and see sky—and be happy to see only sky, instead of wanting it to be some kind of earthmoving, wildly distorted experience all the time?" No one responds.

John Denver was a wise man—that's all I'm saying. I look back at my two friends and smile. "Come on, hurry up and finish that thing—we have to get back before they realize we're gone."

• • •

I kept my thoughts about the woods and the distant suns to myself that night—I didn't share them with anyone, because if I did, it would somehow diminish the beauty of it all.

When I got home the next day, I called Connie. "Hey," I said.

"Hey, how was it?"

"It was everything you said it would be." I paused. "And I didn't."

"I'm smiling big right now," she said.

So was I.

# Chapter 14

Second semester started before I knew it. I was feeling a little better about myself lately. I had sort of turned a new leaf. I know that sounds lame, but I really was trying. As much as I loved what Norma and Ishaan had done for me during my deepest, darkest times, I felt that I had almost outgrown them. All they wanted to do on the weekend was get high.

Go to the movies—get high.

Go to the park—get high.

Watch Netflix—get high.

Connie had really tried hard to put me in a better place, and for that I was grateful. I owed it to her to make an effort. Whenever we talked, or when she came over, it was the first thing she'd ask.

"You haven't been getting high, have you?"

"No," I answered.

"Or drinking."

"No." I was truthful. The only thing that still irked her was the way I dressed. I told her not to judge.

So, things were getting better, but, of course, as soon as my life started to look up, there was always another crisis looming on the horizon.

• • •

One day, I'm sitting with Ishaan in the cafetorium when Norma walks in, her eyes red and puffy. She spots us and ambles over, her apple and water bottle tucked against her chest. She isn't eating much these days, as she thinks she's fat. I beg to differ on that one.

"Hey." I nod to her as she pulls a chair up to the table. "Wut up?"

"My parents." She sits down hard, lets her "lunch" tumble out of her hands, and folds her arms on the table, laying her head down on them. "I hate them. I hate them so much." Her apple rolls across the table and stops precariously close to the edge.

"So? That's news?" Ish tries to make eye contact with her, but she turns her head away. "We all hate our parents."

"What happened?" I ask, eyeing her with caution and wondering if she's sliding into another bad spell.

"The usual," she says stoically. "I get ninety percent on a test, and they ask why I didn't get a hundred. Mom grounds me and hides her diet pills 'cause she figures out I'm taking them.

I try so hard to do my best, but they're never happy." Norma amazes me. She's a total pothead, but an incredibly brainy one. She got top standing in the Cramer Math Test, beating out every other preppy wannabe in the school, and still her parents won't relax.

"No matter what I do, they can never say they're proud— they just make me feel like shit about my hair and my clothes and stuff like that." She's sniffling now, and her back is heaving.

"And they said that if I cut myself again, they're gonna put me in a hospital, because they're scared I'll overdose or hang myself with a belt in my closet or something." She pulls her sleeves down over her hands and buries her face even farther in her arms.

I reach out and squeeze her shoulder. "Come on, Norma." I glance briefly at Ish, encouraging him to do something. "Just do good for yourself. Not for them—do good for you."

"Yeah, who cares," echoes Ish.

She looks up, resting her head on one hand. "Last night they said they want me to go to therapy. They want me to be like everyone else, but I'm not. Maybe I *should* be just like everyone else and say 'screw the homework' and see how they like it then."

I'm not sure what to say to her so I say the only things that come to mind. "Maybe therapy will be good. I saw a counselor a couple times in school. Talking about stuff actually helps sometimes." I lick my lips and hope my next statement will do more good than harm. "Maybe you could try not smoking and drinking and just let your body be on its own for a while.

It's not as hard as you think. You can try, too, Ishaan." Ish's expression doesn't change, but I know that the idea of giving up weed doesn't appeal to him much. He says it helps with the stress he feels coming from home—his dad pushing the tyranny of "normality" on him.

Norma shoots me a wary side-glance. "But it makes me feel good." She wipes her nose on her sleeve. "It helps me."

"How?"

She shrugs. "It makes things tolerable."

"Why?"

"'Cause I don't have to think of anything if I'm high—or wasted."

"But that doesn't solve shit."

Norma's eyes become razor-thin slits. "Well, maybe it does for me." Her voice is edgy and sharp. I know that's my cue for "shut up and mind your own business."

"Okay, then," says Ishaan in an overly optimistic tone. "Let's all relax here." He turns to me. "Faith, it's just weed—and vodka. People are actually prescribed weed for certain diseases. It's not like she's regularly doing meth or something crazy like that."

*No, of course she's not doing meth—my mother did meth. Excuse me for confusing the two. And thanks for making me feel like shit.* "Thanks for that, Ish. I was only trying to help."

As I sit in awkward silence between my two friends, I'm suddenly sad for Norma—yeah, she has parents, a nice house, nice things, but she's even more alone than me. And Ishaan, I love Ishaan, but he follows Norma around like a puppy. I wish he thought more for himself, and I wish that Norma was stronger. I wish that she had someone—like I have my big sister—to hold a mirror up and show her who she is and who she could become.

And then I have a repugnant thought—am I maybe outgrowing my two best friends? Am I actually moving beyond them, beyond their old ideas and interests in favor of my own new ones? Do I find the two people who got me through middle school immature, selfish, and reckless?

• • •

Our conversation ended when the bell rang for last period. We went our separate ways to class and then off to our buses. But that night, something must have gone very wrong at Norma's house, because the next day, she didn't show up at school. Ishaan wasn't in our first class, and when I saw him in the cafetorium, he was shaken up pretty badly. He sat alone at our spot in the caf, looking small and isolated as I walked over to him.

"Oh, Faith," he says, expressionless. "I wanted to text you, but then I thought I should tell you in person—it's Norma." He draws in a deep breath. "She hurt herself last night—really badly. She's in the hospital on suicide watch."

My mouth tries to work, but nothing comes out. *She tried to kill herself.* I feel the air leave my lungs, expelled by the force of the terrible news. *Tried to kill herself.* Ish grabs me under the arm and he steers me toward the nearest chair. *How could she feel so alone, so hopeless that she thought there was no other way out?*

"Are you okay?" asks Ishaan, guiding me to sit down. I shake my head no, unable to get words. Ishaan continues. "Her mom called early this morning from the hospital. They're keeping her there, until she heals up, and then they're holding her for observation."

I nod. Tears tumble down over my cheeks and onto my T-shirt. "What happened?" I ask choking back a sob.

Ish looks at the floor for answers, but finds none. "I don't know. That's all she said. It must have been really bad though, for Norma to do that."

"But I don't get it, Ish. I mean, she's got everything." I can't help but see things from my perspective. Is it really impossible for her to find some small degree of happiness in her want-for-nothing world, while my world is a crappy town house in a subsidized survey in a crappy part of Greenleigh, one of the crappiest places on earth?

"Yeah, well, yesterday when she came into the caf—you knew she was going over the edge—she could have used your support, you know." He can't look at me. Goddamn Ishaan can't look at me, and I just figured out why—he blames me for this.

"What? Are you trying to say that she did this 'cause I told her to try to stop drinking and smoking weed?" How dare he think that I could be responsible for her cutting her veins open?

"Well, you could have—"

"Fuck you, Ishaan!" My chest is heaving. I am hurt to the core. I grab my things and stalk off, letting my hair fall over my face to cover my eyes. It seems an eternity before I get to the girls' washroom, where I hope there's a limited number of occupants. All I want to do is duck into a stall and cry my eyes out in peace.

Sitting on the toilet, I console myself with the fact that there are only a few weeks left until the end of the school year. Typically, I hate school's end, but now I'm looking forward to it.

• • •

As time went on, the news of Norma's "incident" spread through the school, giving rise to sympathetic looks and comments from some, while others only looked at it as fodder for more torture; statements like "Why don't you two freaks do the same, then the school won't smell so bad," or "It's about time she finished what she started," and my personal favorite, "She couldn't even do that right?"

After a while, Ish and I pushed the incident aside and spoke to each other in a civil manner, but only just. I wrestled for a long time with the notion that Norma could think her life was so hopeless that she had no alternative but to end it. Then I remembered the Darkness and how I thought I couldn't bear it if I had to live with it forever.

But Destiny and Connie kept me going. No matter what, I could always rest assured that we were blood and we were tied together beyond any possible untying. I guess Norma had no one, except parents who, she believed, were never satisfied with her. I wasn't sure what else it could be.

# Chapter 15

I was only five months into grade ten when I ran away.

It was an event that, to me, was totally unexpected, because little by little, I had gained the advantage over the Darkness. I thought I was doing better. I had worked hard to get over my mother's death with some help from Connie. I was actually taking care of myself, and I was doing my homework occasionally and attending school on a regular basis, again due to Connie's coaxing. And although Norma's parents had thought better of their regentrification-of-the-downtown-core notion and moved away to rejoin the upper crust urbanites, I still had Ishaan. I could always rely on him to buoy me up if and when I needed it. And for him, I was happy to return the favor. I was proud of myself for the first time in my life.

But when it happened, even the thought of Ishaan waiting

for me the next day at school wasn't enough to keep me from losing my mind in the maelstrom of feelings.

Though I would never admit it to her, Connie was the person in this world I cared about the most. She was the one whose opinion mattered the most, the sister I looked up to. Frustration, abandonment, rejection, and hopelessness, all tied up in a pretty bow fashioned from vodka and cranberry shooters, sent me reeling that night all the way to the side of a highway, half-drunk out of my mind, hitchhiking my way to Toronto.

Many times I have thought about how fortunate I was not to end up in a ditch somewhere, facedown, raped, ice cold, my unseeing eyes open, destined to be a headline in the morning paper. In the worst of times, I've had fleeting thoughts that, in many respects, I may have been better off that way. But, luckily for me, most of the people I encountered were interested only in convincing me to change my ways. I had the look of a girl in her late teens to early twenties. If they'd only known they were dealing with a fifteen-year-old, I'm sure they would have dropped me off at the nearest police station.

• • •

It's January and Connie's birthday is tomorrow. I dial my big sister's number and she picks up the phone.

"Hi, Connie." I crane my neck to check the kitchen clock. Eleven on a Thursday night. "You're not asleep, are you?"

"Hi, and no, I'm not because I'm answering the phone." Her tone is a bit snarky, but I let it go.

"Sorry to call so late, but hey, it's almost your birthday."

"Yeah, I know." She laughs a little but says nothing else.

"Nineteen tomorrow, big sister. Actually, in about an hour…so I wanted to be the first to wish you happy birthday, even though it isn't…quite yet." I wince because I hate the way I sound when I'm rambling. "Feel any different?"

"Nah, not really. Maybe I'll—" A voice interrupts her in midsentence.

"Who is that, Connie?" It's Josephine.

Muffling noises, then Connie's voice from a distance. "It's Faith. She called to wish me a happy birthday."

"Oh, isn't that nice. Why don't you invite her to come over tomorrow night with the rest of your friends. Tell her I said hi." Josie's footsteps fade.

There is dead silence on the other end of the line until Connie takes a deep breath. Then, in a sugary sweet voice, she responds. "Sure, Gran." Then to me, "Did you hear, Faith? I'm having people over tomorrow. Not too many, only twenty or so. Why don't you come over around nine?" Her voice sounds flat.

Afterward, I play the scene over in my mind: My call comes out of the blue, Connie doesn't expect it, Josie walks into the room and says invite your sister to the party you were never going to invite her to. I would not have been invited had it not been for Josie. Even though I know that, I'm still intrigued at being invited to a nineteenth birthday party—and finally meeting some of Connie's friends.

"Okay, that would be great. Thanks." I smile into the handset.

"No problem. Can you get a ride up here?"

"I'll take the bus, no big deal." The more I think about it, the more excited I become. A party at Connie's. She'll be an adult in every way now—able to buy alc. Anyway, I don't care about that—I am going to my big sister's nineteenth birthday party! I can't tell Des, though, because she'd feel left out. This is obviously only for older kids—and despite the fact that in a few weeks I would only turn sixteen, I felt very much in my mind and soul that I was one of them.

"Okay. See you tomorrow, Faith."

"Bye." The line goes dead, but I feel very much alive. More alive than I have in months. I didn't realize how much I missed Norma until that very moment.

• • •

At lunch the next day, Ishaan and I went to the drugstore near the school and scoured the shelves for something unique, finally settling on a purple-streak kit for my now jet-black hair. I loved wild colors, and I was ready for a bold statement.

"You are gonna look on point tonight, Faith," cooed Ishaan.

"This'll look sick with my outfit!"

"Hmm, you're gonna snag yourself a man tonight—I'm jealous. I wish I could go with you."

"Me too, but it's Connie's party, and it's only for people that she's really close to." I felt very important at that moment, and Ishaan's face brightened with a big smile.

We walked back to school, and I couldn't take my eyes off

the clock for the rest of the day. Time crawled by until finally, it was time to go home.

• • •

That night, I warn Gran Dot that I'll probably be sleeping over at Connie's and not to expect me home. I also dodge Des, to avoid having to explain why I'm so dressed up.

Convinced that I look cool beyond words with my purple-streaked hair setting off my brow and lip piercings. I swagger to the bus stop in my black skin-tight jeans and a red and black lumberjack shirt under a parka, garnering lots of head turns on the way. I wait there, cold beyond words by now, with a bare midriff peeking out from under my teeny-tiny crop top. I have to take two buses to get to Connie's house, so I need to board the 7:50 if I want to get there for around nine.

At long last, I catch sight of the Number 55 lumbering along Purdy Street. The operator stops the bus in front of me, opens the doors, then looks me up and down as I board.

I drop the change in the money slot. "Can I get a transfer?" I say gruffly. The driver tears a slip from the holder and hands it to me, staring at my piercings and my hair. I grab it and mumble, "What the frig are you lookin' at." The driver immediately snaps his gaze to the road in front and accelerates, jerking the bus forward, so that I almost fall flat on my ass and make a fool of myself.

The bus jogs along in an endless succession of starts and stops, loading every variety of Friday-night freak and unsavory character along the bus route. I smile as I look out the window into the darkness of the chilly January night. We get downtown, so I buzz and exit. Then, looking focused and straight ahead, I walk confidently to my next destination—Connie's bus. I can't wait to get to her house out in the suburbs.

Riding on the bus, swaying side to side, my thoughts drift to my future and to my little sister's future. She is smart, me not so much. Connie is smart, too, and she has privilege and opportunity. Could I dream?

*It would be great if we could all live together again, me and Connie and Des—all together, like Mom would have wanted. One day, we're gonna make it happen. I'm gonna turn the page, keep turning the pages, study, go to school, and go to college—learn how to cut hair or something and make it happen.* I'm wearing what I know is a stupid grin; Do I care? Hell, no—I am going to my sister's nineteenth birthday party in Irony Heights and I couldn't be happier.

Neely Boulevard flashes on the scroll at the front of the bus. That's Connie's street. I press the buzzer, and soon the bus pulls to a stop. I feel Connie's card tucked into my jacket pocket and think of how she might react to what I have placed in it for her. I made her a bracelet from tiny beads, a really intricate design that I found on YouTube. It has all our names on it—Constance, Faith, Destiny. Actually, I made three; one for each of us. Connie's is purple, her favorite color, mine is red, and Destiny's is green, 'cause she is all environmental. I started them over Christmas break and worked on them so they'd be ready for Connie's birthday. It took me weeks to finish them, but it was worth it, because I know that her rich friends can buy her all kinds of fancy stuff, but this bracelet is one of a kind—correction, three of a kind—LOL!

I get off the bus and start walking the half block or so to Connie's. I can already see activity up ahead. Even though it's cold, people are outside, milling around, with beers and red drink cups in their hands. My stomach tingles with excitement as I walk, crunching the course salt still hanging around from last week's snowfall. I make my way past the five or so guys, who stop talking and gawk at me. On the porch, some uppity chicks stare at me like I have three heads. I let myself in.

Connie's house is jumping. Drake is blaring—not exactly my taste, but this crowd probably hasn't even heard of the bands I listen to. Everyone is drinking, and some people are making out on the couches.

I scan the place for Connie, all the while drawing looks and raised brows from the preppy crowd. Most of the guys are wearing jeans, and the girls are in posh-looking clothes and makeup-store makeup. Truthfully, they all look like clones to me, but whatever. They're Connie's friends so I keep my mouth shut.

I feel a tap on my shoulder and I jerk around. There's Connie, and for a split second, it looks like she's assessing me up and down. Then her face breaks into a grin, and she puts her arms around me. "Hi, Faith!"

"Happy birthday, Connie," I say, pulling the card out of my coat pocket and handing it to her.

"Who's this, Connie?" asks an athletic-looking, thick-necked guy who happens to be standing next to us. He has two beers in his hands and sips from one bottle, then the other.

"This is Faith."

"So this is your sister!" He extends a hand. "Nice to meet you. I'm Matthew."

I do the civil thing and shake his hand, but I don't like him. His smile is fake and he has too many teeth. "Hi." Connie peers at me like she wants me to elaborate, so I add, "Nice to meet you, too."

She pulls me closer and whispers, "Isn't he hot? He's asked me out on a date tomorrow. He's in college."

"Sure," I lie.

"Come 'ere." She takes my hand and leads me down the hallway and into the dining room, where there are fewer people. "Sit here so I can open this—God, I missed you!" Her breath smells like she's had a few, and her speech is a little slurry.

Connie opens the card and catches the bracelet in her lap as it slips out. "Hey, what's this?" She scoops it up and looks at it lovingly. "Oh my God, you made this, didn't you!" Then she reads the inscription—*Big Sister*. She smiles and reads the card.

*Dear Connie,*

*Even though sometimes we don't agree on stuff, I still love you—my big sister. I love talking to you, even though lately it's mostly been on the phone. Hope you like the bracelet. I made one for Des and one for me, too, so we can all have something that's the same. And thanks for all your help and advice. Even though I come off sounding sometimes like you're sticking your nose in my biz, I really don't mean it.*

*Still can't believe you're 19!!!!!!!!*
*Happy b-day! hugzzzzzzzzzz and XXXXXXX....*

*Your sis,*
*Faith*

"Oh my God, Faith," she says as she side-hugs me. "Thank you so much. It's beautiful. Help me put it on."

"Okay, here." I take the bracelet from her and tie the strings around her slender wrist. "See mine?" *Middle Sister.* I show off its triplet, wrapped around my wrist. "They're like the ones we had when we were kids, remember?"

"Oh, yeah! Ooh, I love it!" she coos.

I'm elated and feeling extremely proud of myself. Even if Connie and I have drifted apart for a while, I know that deep in her heart she loves me. "So where's Josephine? Did you kick her out for the night?"

She laughs out loud. "No. She's upstairs in her bedroom, keeping an eye on all the other bedrooms." Connie rolls her eyes and laughs again.

Yeah, she's had a few drinks, that's for sure.

My eyes stray to the French doors behind her, and I notice six or seven girls looking in at us. One of them says something to another girl who snickers. I have a feeling they're not commenting on how cute and sisterly we look. I glance back to Connie and motion toward them. "What the fuck is up with them?" I say, my tone suspicious.

Connie turns around, then peers back at me. "Don't worry

about them." She stands and pulls me up, leading me to another door and heading upstairs. "Come on. Josie will want to say hi to you."

I take a fleeting look back at the giggling blond clones and, honestly, I can't help it. I hold up my hand and give them a one-finger salute.

I hear a chorus of "Oh my God" drawl out as we make our way up to see Josie. I revel in that because shocking people kinda makes me feel good.

"Look who's here, Gran Josie," announces Connie as she opens the door to Josie's bedroom. I walk in behind her and see Josie sitting on her chaise, reading a book. I don't know how she can read with all that pumping music.

"Oh, Faith." Her face looks a little startled. "You colored your hair, I see." She takes off her glasses, gets up, and walks toward me, her arms out. She hugs me and air-kisses my cheek. "And you have more piercings on your pretty face.... Oh, why are you doing that, sweetheart?"

"Hi, Josie." I half-smile at her. She is such a grandma. A typical grandma who can't keep her opinions to herself. And I'll admit, I like her for it, especially since most of the time I'm not sure if my own Gran even cares if I am around or not.

"Sit here and talk awhile—how are things with you? And Destiny, how is she?"

"I'm okay, and Des is doing well. She's really smart and—"

Connie clears her throat and starts backing out of the bedroom. "Hey, Faith, Gran Josie—I'm going to let you two catch up, okay?"

I open my mouth and step to the door, too, wanting to follow her out. "Well, I guess I should—"

"Oh no, Faith, wait," Josie interrupts. "Come sit for a minute or two. I want to talk to you."

I breathe deeply, then surrender to her wishes. Connie winks at me.

"See you downstairs," she says, then turns and closes the door behind her.

# Chapter 16

"Talk to me about you. Are you well?" Josephine looks concerned.

"I guess I'm okay." I sit down beside her on the chaise lounge and shrug, not thinking I was that messed up anymore. "I stopped doing weed and I don't mix drinking with prescription drugs, if that's what you're wondering."

Josephine gives a little start. "Well, that's a good thing, Faith." She smiles. "I'm glad you are living healthier—Connie is proud of your progress—she tells me, you know."

"Yeah—I'm proud of me, too. I mean, you know, sometimes I still have trouble sleeping and stuff, but Connie kept on telling me to think about what I was doing and about where I was going. She made me look inside myself, you know?" I'm pleased to share this with her. "I'm glad I listened because a lot of people I know don't have anyone to tell them to straighten up, and they fall into bad spaces or they let bad stuff fill the spaces that are empty inside them, you know?"

Josie nods. She is really, really listening to what I'm telling her. "Yes, I know." Josie reaches over and puts her hand over mine. "I know, Faith. I think your mom felt those empty spaces." She bites her lip. I look in her eyes and think I see her hesitate. "Your mom was very much in love with Connie's dad. When he died, I don't think she could handle the loss and went into a depression of sorts, trying to find ways to forget. I know she loved you girls so much—her heartache was just too much for her." She stops there and brightens. "But I'm glad you're stronger, dear, and I'm happy you put all that unpleasantness behind you—and I'm happy Connie invited you tonight."

"Me too," I say. Then I give her hand a little squeeze and rise. "I should be getting back to the party." I lean down to kiss her cheek. "See ya, Josie."

"Take care, Faith."

I close the bedroom door behind me and sigh. Could this night be any better?

My heart is light and I feel—loved. Yes—I will allow that. And it is time to celebrate with my sister. And though I'm not looking forward to running the gauntlet through all the preppies, I do want to get my hands on a drink and also look for Connie.

My feet skip down the winding staircase, dodging the few bodies who are milling about at the bottom of the steps, engaging in the social dance of teen binge drinking. Some are already staggering, being obnoxious and stupid; some are being led out the door to a waiting taxicab, probably going to a friend's house for the night to sleep it off and call Mommy or Daddy in the morning for a ride home.

I make a beeline for the kitchen, where I hit the jackpot. There's a sink full of ice, into which is jammed a plethora of beers, sodas, and vodka coolers. On the counter sits an abandoned tray of Jell-O shots, red as candy apples, just waiting to be shot back. I grab a couple and down one right away. When it sinks nicely into my belly, I blast the second one to the back of my throat. I set the empties on the counter and grab a can of beer, open it, and take a big sip. I am off to a good start. I sip again.

Now to find Connie. I'm beginning to feel a nice warmth inside. I walk around the house at a leisurely pace, observing the people Connie chooses to hang with these days and come to an inevitable conclusion—they're all cookie-cutter kids just looking to fit in to the rich-kid mold. I would have expected people with a little more substance, a bit more intelligence and character. But if that's who Connie wants to hang with, who am I to comment? I take more sips and finish up the beer, so I go back and get another.

The music is loud, and now there are more people in the house, if that's possible. This was a little get-together? I'm having trouble keeping up with what is happening around me. I feel warm—then someone appears.

"Hey." A big guy is swaying in front of me with a beer bottle in his hand.

"Hey," I echo.

"Is that your real hair color?" He has a stupid grin on his face and his tone is mocking.

"Yeah," I reply. "And my pee is purple, too."

At this, he hoots out a loud laugh. "Hey, you're funny. Connie's sister, right?"

I jerk my head back, 'cause in addition to beer breath, he's slurring his speech badly and spitting all over me. "Yeah. Have you seen her?" I take a sip.

"Who?"

*Are you kidding me?* "Connie," I say, rolling my eyes.

"Uh, yeah, she's in the sunroom, I think." He lifts his beer hand and points, slopping beer onto the floor. "It's back there."

"I know where the sunroom is," I say in a snarky tone. "I've been here before, lots of times."

"Hey, you're a feisty little bitch, aren't you!"

I hate that word. With every cell of my body, I hate that word. I whirl around and push my face into his, spilling some of my drink on his shirt.

"Don't you dare call me a bitch, you brainless jock." His face splits into a big stupid grin. I want to kick him in the ass, but I think maybe that wouldn't be such a good idea, because he looks how I figure Goliath must have looked. Even though I am tipsy, I can still make a judgment call. So I down my drink, turn on my heel, and continue my quest for Connie.

I feel his belittling, critical eyes following me as I approach the sunroom doors, and that bothers me.

Maybe if I'd acted on my anger toward him, I would have

turned and created a scene, after which Connie would surely have either come to my rescue or admonished me for my sins against her precious friends. In any event, I wish, above all other wishes, that I had done something different. I should have stomped in and declared my presence; anything besides walking to those sunroom doors at that very moment and just standing there like an idiot, because what happened next changed everything.

# Chapter 17

As I approach, I see the top of Connie's head poking up from behind the enormous wicker couch in the center of the room. Several of her Barbie doll friends sit around her like she's the queen bee. This room is away from the living room, where the music is blaring—another twist of fate. If she'd been anywhere else in the house, her words probably would have been drowned out by The Weeknd's latest single blasting away.

"Oh my God, like, does she think she's a hipster with that skanky look of hers?" says one of them, with disdain in her voice. My mind races as I hang back in the shadow of the doorway.

"Like, I feel so fucking bad for you, Connie—what's wrong with her?" asks another, her tone sickeningly sympathetic. The realization that they are talking about me sweeps over me like a tidal wave.

"God," huffs Connie.

I feel a glow of anticipation as I wait for her response. *Tell them, Connie. Tell them they are fucking losers and to get the hell out of your house, and how dare they talk about your sister like that, those bony-assed, white-trash nasty things.*

"I don't know. She's not on drugs anymore, which is good, I guess."

*Wait, that's not telling them to shut up and get out of your house—that's kind of like agreeing with them.*

"Shit. What that took on my part, I can't even tell you. It was like I had to convince her, you know—actually, like, beg her to stop. I was drained emotionally after talking to her sometimes—like, so bad." Connie places her hand on her forehead, like she's suffering great hardship.

A surreal clarity washes over me—like I'm standing outside my body, watching myself listen to my sister trash-talk me with her slurred drunken speak. My sister, breaking a sister's unspoken covenant and stabbing me in the back with these strangers, fueling their condescending, snooty judgment on me. I can't move. So I just listen—the worst thing I can do, because there's more.

"I feel for you, Connie. It must be so hard for you."

"Yeah. Like, is she in a group home or something?"

"No, she's still living with her grandmother in the DC."

"Oh my God, the DC—I've heard about that. It's, like, right in the middle of, like, gangs and stuff."

"Oh my God, she lives there?"

"Like, she's still my sister, and I feel so sorry for her. I really feel like she's had a lot to deal with and all, but everyone knows not to do prescription drugs, right? Like, really? Her grandmother called here and she was going nuts with her—I had to, like, talk to her and shit all the time. She finally stopped and turned herself around, I guess. And my little sister is just on the brink of being affected by her—thank God she's got more brains than Faith."

I actually feel a heaviness in my chest when she speaks my name in amongst all that toxic babble. My breathing becomes shallow.

"And what's with her hair? Those cheap, purple streaks— she looks like my dog when Mom brings him home from the groomer and she's put a blueberry wash in his fur." A peel of giggles reverberates from the couch. I feel like someone has taken a jackhammer to my head.

After Connie recovers from her bout of laughter at my expense, she speaks up again. "I think she did that 'cause she knows my favorite color's purple. Look what she made for me." Her head inclines, and my guess is that she's pointing out the bracelet. They all gawk at it.

"Cute," says one of them.

"You'd never know she was your sister, though, Connie," says another. "You guys are like night and day."

"Yeah, what the hell?"

"She's got a different dad—not even sure who he was." Connie shakes her head. "Thank God I had at least one normal parent."

"Come on, Connie, you must have some of her mother in you, too," one of them says, egging her on.

"Oh please—I knew long ago that my mother was fucked up. I don't want to be in any way associated with that screwup." This is the worst of all. "Sometimes I wish I was an only child. It would be easier that way—not having sisters and worrying about their potential fuckups for the rest of my life—not having to think of one day bailing them out of jail or whatever." The others nod to show they concur with her.

I'm stunned. My whole life, the only solid foundation upon which anything lasting could be built, has crumbled right out from under me. I am alone—completely and utterly alone. My big sister is a lie—as elusive as a shadow.

Then, after a pause, "Do you want another drink?" Connie is starting to get up. "This is, like, bringing me down."

I back away into the middle of the house, into the noise, into a corner. I can't think of what to do next. I'm too angry to cry, yet too hurt to lash out at anyone. My thoughts blow around in my mind like leaves in a storm. Everything I thought I knew about Connie is lost—so I'm lost, too. *I need a drink.*

The beer is still working its way around my system, but I need something to take the edge off my emotions. With half-empty cups all over, I can have my fill of whatever is lying around, so I just grab one and drink, then grab another and finish that, too. Then another. When I finish the last one, I feel a sloshy fullness in my stomach that warns me I've reached well over what should have been my limit.

"You never know how strong you are until being strong is your only choice." Bob Marley said that.

*Now, get out, Faith. Run. Get the hell out of here and keep on going.* The voice in my head sounds like it knows what I should do. I calmly put down the empty cup and walk toward the front door, pushing past the activity around me. *There's nothing here for you.* Near the door, I spot a leather jacket, a nice black leather jacket, just thrown on a chair, so I grab it and put it on in one swift motion.

I don't bother to close the door behind me. I walk from the house in the cold darkness of this January night, and sharp, clear pictures come to me. They are images of my sisters and my mother and me, living together again, happy. The thoughts make me cry, so I brush them away along with the tears that streak my face.

Approaching the bus stop, I feel a desperation I've never felt before, even in my darkest times. Being alone in a crowd of people is about as alone as you can be. That's how I feel tonight.

The drinks are getting to me now—my stomach is turning. I stick my hands in the jacket pockets and feel something in one of the them. A wallet. I open it up, still striding to the bus stop—twenties—lots of them. I stop and count: seven, eight, nine, ten twenties. Two hundred dollars, thank you very much. I count again. Yes, it really is two hundred dollars in my hands.

*What can I do with this? Get the hell out of here. Get the hell out—fuck 'em all. I'll go to Toronto—take the bus. But then I have to spend some of this on bus fare. Screw that. I'll hitch a ride.*

I take a step to the bus stop, but don't make it. I lean into someone's hedges and heave out a red mix of cranberry juice, beer, and whatever else I've gulped down. Coughing and gagging, still holding on to the wallet and money with one hand and my hair with the other, I take in steady breaths to try to stop the heaving.

When I get my bearings back, I straighten up, wipe my chin, and spit out what's left of the acidy bile in my mouth. Then, devoid of any dignity, I walk to the stop and tear my triplet bracelet off my wrist as I wait. The Number 4 bus back to downtown Greenleigh appears first as two small lights in the distance. It draws closer and closer until it pulls up to the curb, with a squeal of brakes. The doors open and I look up at the driver. It's an older woman.

"You okay there, hon?" She asks so sweetly that I feel like I am going to cry again. Holding on to the grab bar, I board and throw some change into the fare box.

"Yeah, I'm fine." I stagger to a seat at the back and pray to the Ultimate Being that I don't vomit again. The rocking motion of the bus isn't helping, so I open up a window and gulp down mouthfuls of cold air. In spite of being hammered, my mind is working pretty clearly.

I am not going to the bus stop in downtown Greenleigh to catch the connecting bus back to Danziger Crescent. I'm not going to crawl back and live out a miserable existence knowing that the one person whom I thought held out a glint of hope for me thinks I'm a joke. Anger seethes in me. I want to tear everything apart, starting with Connie, because she's the one who has torn out my soul. I hate my mother, my grandmother, and I hate the Ultimate Being. I want to take down the world because I wasn't the one sitting on a big couch in a sunroom in

Irony Heights surrounded by everything a person could ever want. *Why wasn't I the one—why?*

There's no way I'm going back home, because there's nothing to go home to. Destiny will be okay without me. Connie said I'm nothing but a bad influence on her. This is better for me, better for Destiny, and obviously better for Connie. It's clear that she's embarrassed to have any association with me at all. The only person I can think of who would miss me is Ishaan, but I know he will be okay, too; he's stronger than me and Norma put together.

The bus finally rolls to the stop, and my thoughts have to wait; it's time for strategy now. *Bye, nice bus driver—too bad I'll never see you again.* I stride determinedly down the four blocks to the Toronto off-ramp, choose a strategic spot where as many cars as possible will see me, and stick my thumb out to hitch a ride. I know that hitching is dangerous and stupid and all that, but for me, it's leave or die trying.

The guy who picks me up on the side of the highway is some kind of religious freak, and looking back, I consider this one of my most fortunate moments. I think he was probably a born-again Christian who saw me as an opportunity to garner a convert.

"Where are you headed?" he asks.

"I need to get to Toronto," I slur. He looks me in the eye. "No, I'm going back home to Toronto. My ride bailed on me, and I have no money to get a bus."

"Yeah, whatever." He shakes his head. "Get in."

I open the door and half-fall into the seat.

His name is Reggie. Balding, middle-aged, and skinny, he looks like a creeper but he turns out to be a nice guy.

"You been drinking?" he asks.

"Yeah."

"You know that's not good for you."

"I don't care—maybe I'll die. No one would care anyway."

"You're running away, aren't ya?" he asks with narrow eyes.

"No, I told you I missed my—my ride bailed on me." Lies are hard to remember when you're wasted.

"Okay, you're not running away, but just in case…"

He talked about salvation and the need to repent almost the entire way to Toronto. Then he even gave me some suggestions on where to go to keep warm and to stay away from trouble—that was a little weird—like he knew exactly what he was talking about.

"You can always panhandle for extra money," says Reggie matter-of-factly. "Being young and a girl, you should always stay near somewhere public, like a library, or a big store, in case someone tries to kidnap you. A general rule of thumb: If someone tells you they'll give you a room for the night, say no. There's no such thing as a free lunch. And don't sleep in a park; you could get yourself killed or somethin'. Sleep in a doorway, near somewhere that stays open all night and is lit up so you don't get raped or mugged. College campuses are the main safe places, 'cause the buildings are usually open around the clock and will offer you shelter. But look the part with a notebook and some kinda text book. They have campus patrol officers who'll see you and be suspicious. Janitors will turn you in if you're sleeping in an area where they have to clean. And you might want to check an Internet café to research runaway shelters, and visit a mall, or a mission, or a public library for warmth. And for heaven's sake, if you ever need help, go to a church or to the police, no foolin' now."

My head is reeling as I try to set his instructions in my mind and remember them all. I can't believe I'm actually doing this. I feel empowered, defiant.

In the end, I promise I'll be careful. Reggie wishes me well and gives me twenty bucks after he drops me off in front of one of the University of Toronto libraries. I thank him and wave good-bye.

I search out a bathroom on one of the top floors and lock the door. Then I rinse out my mouth, wash my face with foamy soap from the dispenser, and slide down to the floor.

I panic and think I maybe did the wrong thing. *What am I doing? All I have to do is go to Union Station and catch a train home. I have the money, and if I leave now, I can be home before anybody notices I'm missing.*

*But is that what I want? I have to think about it clearly— now isn't the time. Maybe tomorrow.... I'll decide tomorrow.*

With these thoughts running through my head, I settle down and fall asleep with two hundred and twenty dollars in my pocket, and spotty hopes for the morning.

# Chapter 18

I convince myself that my gut feeling was right—I'll try to build a life here, away from who I was in Greenleigh. I'm going to look for a place and find a job, and when I make something of myself, I'm going back to prove to everyone that I'm not a loser from the DC, but a woman who made it on her own, without help from her rich grandmother.

Thrift stores are great for cheap necessities, so I buy a backpack, warm sweaters, and sweatpants. Then I go to a dollar store for a toothbrush, toothpaste, spare undies and soap. I spend only forty bucks, which leaves quite a bit for food, for a little while at least. Living on the street the first few days isn't horrible, because I have things to do, but after awhile, the monotony of surviving becomes boring. Plus, the janitors at the university are on to me, so I have to clear out and find another place to sleep.

Obviously, winter is a harsh time for homeless people, because with the cold, you're dealing with the possibility of hypothermia, frostbite, and freezing to death. A street kid I talk to suggests a youth shelter on Sanger Street, just off Yonge. But he warns me that when it's this cold, they fill up fast and some have to make do outside. That's a frightening thought. I picture some random person finding me, a human Popsicle, in the morning. The shelter is where I head—so far, so good. One week on the street. I'm still not in trouble and I'm still alive.

• • •

"All residents must follow some basic rules and live up to certain expectations," says the lady at the desk. I've already registered with my name and fake date of birth at the intake desk. Now I'm trying to concentrate on the rules and expectations as this woman rambles on. "While at Sanger Street Shelter, or Triple-S House, this includes being respectful to others, keeping your bed space clean, and looking for work and housing. If you have other responsibilities—for example, attending school or performing community service hours—then we can assist you with that. Does that apply to you?"

"Uh, no." She blinks at me looking like she's assessing my sincerity. "I just need a place to stay for a while, until I find a job and an apartment."

"Okay. What's your name again?"

"Norma."

"Norma. You're lucky you got a bed tonight—it's cold out there." She sticks out her hand and I shake it. "My name's

Katherine. I'm a counselor here. If you're ready, I'll take you to your bed." As she leads me up the stairs, a variety of noises comes from inside the other rooms. She raps on one door and says, "Keep it down in there—remember the rules."

Then she turns to me. "Breakfast is served at seven, continental style. We have bread, buns, juice, fruit, and cereals. A bag lunch is provided to all who sign up for one—sometimes a hot lunch is provided, but that depends on availability of staff. You can ask for a single room if you have to get up early for work or if you're pregnant. Are you pregnant?"

"No."

"That's good. Triple-S is not long-term housing. We work with residents to find appropriate housing that is clean, safe, and affordable, but generally people are expected to find housing within six weeks. There's lockers in the main area if you have any valuables. Any questions?" It sounds like she's been through this a million times.

"No."

She comes to an open door. There's a girl with mousy brown hair, lying spread-eagle on one of the beds. "Sarah, this is Norma. Norma, Sarah. All right, Norma, if you need anything, let me know." Katherine points down the hall. "Bathroom's over there. And remember, clean up after yourself. Good night." She turns and heads back downstairs. I feel a little uncomfortable, being left with this emo-looking thing who appears to be on the brink of committing suicide.

Sarah moves her head to look at me. "My name's not really Sarah, it's Emma."

I smile. "And my name's not really Norma, it's Faith."

She props herself up on her elbow. "Where are you from?"

"Greenleigh. You?" I walk into the room.

"Sioux Lookout."

"Where's that?"

"Northern Ontario—between Thunder Bay and Winnipeg, Manitoba."

"How did you get here?" I ask, placing my backpack on the bed.

"I ran away with my boyfriend, but he dumped me, and now I don't have any money to get home." She lies back down and looks at the ceiling. "Not even sure I wanna go home, you know. It's messed up. Why are you here?"

"'Cause everyone in my family hates me," I say with disdain.

"I can relate." She sighs and turns over on her bed. "Okay, I'm going to sleep now. Maybe we can talk more tomorrow."

I pick up my backpack, walk to the bathroom, and take the longest shower in history, hoping to wash the streets off me before I sleep in a bed for the first time in a week. I debate for a while whether or not to use the lockers for my money, but I decide to keep it in my panties instead—I find it hard to trust anyone right now. I can't believe that people live for years on the streets. I am not cut out for it.

The next morning, I do talk to Emma. We speak casually over our breakfast of Raisin Bran, orange juice, and yogurt.

"Where are you going today?" she asks.

"Not sure," I reply. "I'm going to try to look for a job."

"Are you coming back here tonight?" She looks around at the other residents sitting haphazardly around the dining room.

"Probably. Why?"

Emma leans in over the table and talks really quietly. "I crashed here last night 'cause it was too far to go to where I usually stay, and I didn't have spange for the bus. Spare change," she explains, when I look bewildered. She leans in closer and whispers, "I got mugged last night, while trying to score some H, the fuckers. They took all the money I panhandled yesterday."

*Score some H.* That sounds like serious drugs. I decide I should react like it is no big deal. "That sucks," I say, like I've heard her story a thousand times.

"You bet your ass it sucks. I mean, it's baby stuff for me, not anywhere near King Kong or anything, you know—I just needed it."

I nod. I know that means she is an occasional drug user not a straight-out addict. "You were trying to score heroin?"

"Yeah."

I raise my brows slightly, then look away. I think of Reggie and his warning. Then I think of Connie, and my Gran and my mother, and I wonder what the hell am I doing here.

"You use?" she whispers, pushing her cereal away.

"No, not since last year," I say in a normal voice, then taking a small bite of cereal. "I was a baby user. Kiddie drugs, weed." I shrug as I chew. "Want to keep away from that shit. My mom died from meth—messed her up really bad."

"I hear you. This place, though, that I sleep at sometimes—Brian's okay. He won't bother you or anything. He deals but only on the side. He has a repair store, and sometimes he doesn't make enough, so he gets stuff from his brother, who, like, deals hardcore, and then he sells the stuff to make his rent."

I nod. *Why is she telling me this?* The hair on my neck stands on end. "Thanks, but…I don't need to crash there. I'm gonna stay here for a while and look for a job, try to find a place." I don't tell her that I have a hundred and eighty dollars tucked in between two pairs of underwear, both of which I am wearing.

"Sure," she says. "Well, I gotta go. I'm heading to Brian's. Hey, if you change your mind—" She gets up and reaches for a pad of paper and a pen sitting on a desk near the phone. "I'll write his address for you in case things don't work out. Brian's okay with letting my friends couch surf. I think he kinda likes me."

I raise my brows. She slides the paper over to me, and, after hesitating a moment, I pick it up and look at the address, not that I know where it is or anything. I fold it neatly and place it in my jeans back pocket.

"Thanks for that, Emma. And…that's great for you—that you always have a place to go." I try to think of something positive to say about an obviously effed-up situation. Not that I am in a better situation myself, you understand.

"Yeah," she says, after which an uncomfortable silence hangs in the air, our eyes looking everywhere but at each other. We have run out of things to say. She rises, straightens her jeans, and zips up her jacket. "I guess I should go and make some money." She grabs her satchel. "Don't lose that address, just in case."

"Thanks. I won't." Emma leaves the dining room and signs out, waving to the day counselor at the desk. I never see her again.

• • •

I spend the day in and out of stores in the neighborhood, asking if I can fill out applications, using the Triple-S House address as my residence, which may not have been a good idea. I even take my piercings out and throw them away so I look more normal. I am ready to take on the world and show everyone how wrong they were about me, especially Connie.

The next night, I go back to Triple-S and am assigned to a different room, with a different girl. Her name is Katy—at least she says it is. She seems nice enough, and we start chatting about her dad and the fact that he was abusive to her mom and that she left because she couldn't take his behavior anymore; he was turning on her, too.

After we talk, I head to the shower, taking all my stuff with me, removing the money from my panties, and putting it in my backpack until I can redo the double-panty thing after my shower. The hot water feels good, warming me all over, taking the grit from the car exhaust out of my hair. After toweling down, I fetch my sweats and slip them on, ready to sleep off the long day of walking, trying to find a job.

When I get back to the room, Katy is already asleep, so I place my backpack and jacket at the foot of my bed, forgetting all about the panty thing, and crawl into bed. I think about tomorrow and the fact that I have to do this all over again. Living on my own isn't as glamorous as I thought it would be. I tell myself that all I need in life is to land a minimum-wage job and find a cheap place to live—a basement apartment shared with others will do me just fine right now, and maybe work myself up from a minimum-wage position to manager. With these thoughts occupying my head, I go from a bazillion miles an hour to out cold in no time, exhausted beyond words.

• • •

Did I say that Katy seemed nice? Yeah, well, scratch that. *Seemed* is the operative word here—she was no Emma.

When I wake up the next morning, my leather coat is gone, along with my one hundred and eighty dollars—that lying, thieving lowlife took my money and my jacket—well, what had become my jacket and what had become my money. I messed up and was caught off guard, which cost me plenty—a nice warm coat and my cash reserve.

Enraged and in tears, I rush down to the front desk and hiccup my story to the lady sitting there.

"She took my money and my coat," I shriek, pointing upstairs. "That stealing piece of crap that you put me with last night!"

She stands up and comes around to my side. "Calm down. What happened?"

"That girl in my room—Katy—I woke up this morning and my money was gone—out of my backpack. A-a-and so was my coat." I wipe my nose with the back of my hand.

"I'm sorry about that. It happens sometimes. You could have asked us to hold on to it for you—give it back to you in the morning."

"What do I do now! That's my money!"

"Look, if she ever comes back, we'll call the police, but don't hold your breath." She shakes her head. "She wouldn't be stupid enough to return. I'm sorry." She purses her lips and looks deep in thought. "I think I can help you. Wait here."

In a few minutes, she comes back with the ugliest coat ever made. "I found a parka from a bin in one of the closets." Pleased as punch, she hands me a foul, puky green parka that looks like it could have been worn by a giant. "This should do the trick."

I look at it and frown. "Thanks." I suppose beggars can't be choosers, as Gran would say. Man, did she get that right. I had hoped that when I ran out of money, I could get a quick buck by selling the leather jacket. Now, that backup plan is screwed. Yeah, okay. That jacket and money was taken from someone, but it was a fair take. All he had to do was ask Mommy or Daddy for a replacement and it would happen the next day. But me? Taking from me? From someone who's got nothing? I mean, even if you're another guest at a shelter, there's gotta be some kind of an understood code about that shit. It just should not happen. The rage and dejection I feel are all too familiar. I battled these feelings when I was a kid. I thought that I had overcome the worst of them, but time and fate had other plans.

# Chapter 19

I coasted through the rest of the winter, totally broke, by staying in downtown shelters and drop-in centers, one step ahead of frostbite and hypothermia. My sixteenth birthday came and went without fanfare. I would find shelters, much like Triple-S House, where I would stay for a few days and then move on to the next one, as I didn't take much to their approach on assisting me with getting back to school; I didn't want that, or family mediation or even applying for social assistance. I was too afraid that someone would send me home. Though the last thing I wanted was to be sent back to Greenleigh, I craved a stable home, some place I could call safe, but I also wanted to stay anonymous, be on my own, and live life on my own terms. I was living a dichotomy.

I kept trying to find a job but it was impossible; no one

would hire me once I gave them the address of the shelter in which I was staying at the moment. So I panhandled—on the street, in doorways, and outside of fast-food restaurants—wherever there was a high turnover of people.

One of the things that struck me most was how passersby, people who essentially looked like respectable professionals, felt perfectly free to direct negative and disparaging comments my way. I panhandled anyway. And instead of spending my precious money on food, I would eat at homeless shelters and drop-in centers a couple of times a day. When it was really cold, there were mobile vans that drove around and distributed blankets and food and hot coffee. Some days, I felt like a caveman or something, because my attention and energy were constantly focused on finding a source of food so I wouldn't be hungry. And the amount of food was never enough 'cause I spent all my time and energy looking for it.

Laundry and maintenance stuff was another issue. When my clothes got dirty, I changed in public washrooms and then took them to a Laundromat—not often though, because that cost money. Most of the time, I washed them at a shelter when I stayed overnight. If they started to poke around and ask questions about what my story was, that was my signal to clear out; they had me in their data base.

As the weather got milder, life on the street began to jump. And it wasn't only kids, it was all kinds of people. Unemployed people, people with mental health issues, people with alcohol and drug addictions all poured onto the streets to claim their spots like squirrels and bears coming out of hibernation.

I figured it would be easier in the warmer weather. I ran in circles…circles of friends, circles of fellow runaways, and circles of lost, confused children, even living at a mall for a few weeks in the summer because it was too hot to stay on the street in the daytime. While I stayed at the mall, I met up with two girls who looked like they were trying to be equally inconspicuous, though the giant backpacks gave them away. Taylor and Shaylee were their names. Both of them had backstories that would take the jade off of any social worker.

I met them in the coffee shop bathroom on the third floor of the Eaton Centre one morning, toting large backpacks and sleeping bags. It's a funny thing about street kids. We recognize each other as street kids, even if we're having a particularly good day and not looking so much like a scruffy mess. And, of course, after introductions, which are usually minimal, the inevitable topic of conversation is why you ran away.

After I told them my sad little account of life according to Faith, I asked what was up with them.

"I'll go first," announces Taylor. She's taller than Shaylee by about six inches, with dark hair and eyes but creamy white skin—she reminds me of a streetwise Snow White. "I've been living on the street for two years, give or take a month. My sister and me lived with Mom and Dad until about four years ago, until we were taken away by social services 'cause Mom had us set up on her computer for kiddie porn—both me and my sister, who was, like, only seven when they busted her. Dad knew about it but didn't do much to stop her."

Parents can be sick fucks sometimes.

Shaylee tells me she ran away from an abusive home. "I would get beaten for anything. When I was fourteen, I ran away from my house, 'cause my mom was on drugs and hit me. My dad was physically *and* sexually abusive. I was the only child, and there was no one to protect me, or even to talk to about what was happening. I was so afraid of my parents that I isolated myself from everyone."

"Oh my God, that totally sucks," I say. I had it easy compared to a lot of the kids I was meeting.

"Yeah," agrees Shaylee. "It was only a matter of time before they ended up killing me one day."

I nod sympathetically. "So how do you guys make money? Do you—you know, stroll?"

"I've thought about it sometimes," says Taylor. "You know, when I can't get any spange. On a good day I can get about forty bucks."

"I have a spot downtown where I can make fifty an hour," says Shaylee. "But I try and respect the spot and not go too often. Selling marijuana is a good way to make loads, too, if you know someone who can get it for you. You have to buy it from them and then sell it to tourists. Tourists can pay two or three times more than a local." She takes a sip of her chocolate milk, then looks at me with somber eyes. "But working the street—I dunno—I'd have to be really desperate."

Taylor and Shaylee were my circle for a while, because street life is a transient life and you never know who is going to be there in the morning. And though I was seldom alone, I felt lonely. There were always people who were willing to band together because it was safer in numbers. If you didn't have numbers, then at night, if you couldn't get to a shelter, you didn't sleep—it was just too dangerous to let yourself get vulnerable like that. So I learned that if you're alone, sleeping during the day is better, and keeping your eyes open at night will bring you into the next day. So far I had managed to stay away from drugs and hadn't been sexually assaulted, but I knew deep down that, by the end of this, I wasn't going to be the same.

• • •

Before long, the winds blow colder, the sky is steel gray, and leaves are turning color. Shaylee and Taylor and I are hanging out in the park when some of the guys we met on the street come up to us. We aren't best friends or anything; we just kind of hang out together whenever our worlds collide. They've made enough money to buy some cheap whisky and some pot.

"We got a couple bottles of Wiser's and some ganja. You girls wanna come and party with us?" says the guy named Trevor. He looks like he's just won the lottery or something. "There's an empty factory down by the tracks. Nobody ever goes there." Trevor has a strong chin and aquiline nose—not a pretty face but one that stands out in a crowd.

My friends and I exchange glances and then shrug. "Okay," we say not quite in unison.

"Where and when?" asks Shaylee, acting like she really doesn't care if they answer the question.

"Meet you here when it gets dark—we'll take you."

I admit I'm kind of excited about it. The last time I partied was on my sister's nineteenth birthday—and though that turned out to be a hot mess, I'm ready to escape the general crappiness of being a homeless person by doing a little ganja and downing some drinks.

Anyway, we make our way back to the park after making a stop to a mall washroom and getting cleaned up a little. We give ourselves a cursory wash at the sinks, brush our hair, and then change into the clean clothes we have in our backpacks. I feel good fixing myself up for something.

"You know, I'm kinda psyched for this," says Taylor as we hurry to the park. The sun is a pink sliver on the horizon, peeking through the last of the clouds rushing by the Toronto skyline. An October wind is picking up, a sobering reminder of my days spent battling the elements last January and February.

"Crap, we're early," Taylor huffs, looking at the sun's aura still lingering in the western sky. "We'll probably have to wait awhile before they show."

We get to the park and round the corner to meet up at the bench under the bridge, but what I see makes my blood run cold. There are about six or seven guys, bouncing off each other and acting rough and goofy, like they are already hyped up on something. Scrappy, skinny, and loud, they turn when they see us coming down the incline, our knapsacks bobbing on our backs. I get a bad feeling, the kind where the hairs on your body stand at attention and you get all tingly.

"Yes," hisses Taylor. "They're already here."

"Hi, guys," coos Shaylee.

"'Sup!" Trevor tilts his head toward us and smiles devilishly.

The fact that I'm excited about tonight and that I think he's kinda cute is overshadowed by the reality that this is now a gang as opposed to an even three for three.

"So these are my brothers, ladies," he says, motioning to the two familiar boys. "Kyle and Justin you remember from before." Then he points out to the group behind him, rattling off names. One of them has music blaring out of an iPod, really loud, and I think, *Wow—someone somewhere must be missing that toy—freshly taken 'cause it still has juice.*

"Shit, I don't know about this," I whisper in Taylor's ear.

"Don't be a pussy," she snaps, not even bothering to turn her head toward me. "It'll be fine." I wish I shared her confidence, because I feel like I'm about to be the main course at feeding time in a shark tank.

"Let's go, my ladies, we don't wanna be late for the party." Trevor sounds nice enough. As we walk, he jokes and talks with Taylor. He walks a walk that you have to practice for hours in a mirror in order to be able to achieve that height of swagger. His jeans hang low around his hips and reveal a gray pair of boxers; they're not really looking like they've been freshened up in the last few days or so—but I don't care. I've seen worse, a lot worse.

Shaylee and I fall back with the other boys. She finds conversing easy, while I'm shy and mostly look at the pavement, letting her do the talking. They ask her the usual things kids ask each other: Where are ya from? Why'd you run? What kind of shit do you do? I just listen, smile nervously, and nod from time to time.

We walk for a long time, and finally come to the factory;

abandoned and nondescript, it could have been out of a creepy movie with its broken windows and chained-up door. Like those are really gonna keep us out.

"We can get in this way," says Trevor. He's still up ahead with Taylor. That kinda makes me pissed. Taylor and Trevor, Trevor and Taylor—damn.

We all follow them through the smashed garage door. Its glass panes have been gauged out to allow for easy entry by squatters. There's a few meth heads passed out in the shadows, sleeping off their highs. An image of my mother flashed into my head for a split second as I looked down at them, then just as quickly, I shook it off.

"Over there." Trevor motions to the stairs at the far end of the shop. They look like they lead to an office above the factory floor. "It's more private up there." It's obvious they have partied here before, maybe even stayed here.

We giggle as we follow them into the office. I imagine people worked at manufacturing some nut or bolt or widget here years ago. Now the place has fallen to a bunch of meth heads and runaway teens as their recreation and party room. I can see the ghosts of the workers' disapproving looks in my mind's eye.

A few swigs into the party and after sharing a huge joint with the others, I feel very relaxed. My emotions crystallize inside my head—I've kept them at bay for so long, not letting myself be affected by all the shit that's going down around me, I've gone almost numb. But the chill-out feeling takes me back to a time I didn't have to think about survival.

I see Trevor standing with Taylor, but Taylor is more interested in Kyle, who has an obvious good look about him—of course, she falls for the obvious. Trevor sees me looking at him.

As he walks over amidst the flurry of bodies drinking, smoking, and dancing to a stranger's dying iPod playlist, he drinks and takes a drag from his joint. Trevor puts his hand on my cheek and pulls me close, wrapping his mouth around mine, and blows the musky, hot smoke into my mouth. I inhale it, like I'm inhaling his very essence. As the smoke leaves my mouth, I look at him for what feels like forever—I feel his face with the palm of my hand, until he takes it and puts it on his crotch.

Then I hear a scuffle and look beyond him. It's Shaylee. She is falling down all over the place, and some of the guys are pushing her onto an old drafting table covered in rat shit and dust. She's too drunk to say no—or yes. Her eyes are closed but she has her hands up, flailing around. I look at her with a detached apathy and calmness, thinking that maybe my gut feelings were right.

I open my mouth wider, putting my tongue into Trevor's mouth, but he recoils and falls back, off-balance. It looks like Trevor is dizzier and more drunk than I am, but he's stronger, and he sways back to me, grabbing both my hands, holding them over my head. Another boy comes over to us, a blond boy with transparent skin, and opens my shirt, while Trevor watches.

I feel hands on me. Everything around me slows to a crawl—I wonder where Taylor is and why I can't see her. Then my gaze meanders to an office on the far side with frosted glass partitions, pieces cracked and broken. There's a figure on a table or a desk, not sure which, with shadowy figures around it, like wolves feeding on a fresh kill.

As slow as my mind was working moments before, it accelerates in a flash and brings me into the reality of what all this is leading to.

*Get out—get out—get out!*

Just like that, everything speeds up. My reflexes, my thinking, my body flip into survival mode. My head hits Trevor hard on the mouth, and while he's trying to regain his balance, his crotch gets far enough from me that I have a clear shot, a real hard, deep one. The other boy is in such shock from what I did to Trevor, or maybe he's only too drunk or too stoned, that he stands there, his mouth gaping, for a split second—and that's all I need. Spotting my backpack, I sprint to grab it. The blond boy takes hold of my jacket, and my head jerks, but there's nothing holding me back—'cause I slip my arms out, turn around, grab my backpack, and swing it squarely into his face. He grunts and falls with a thud to the wooden plank floor.

I think seriously about helping Taylor and Shaylee for about a tenth of a second, but I'm too scared. Trevor's holding on to his precious crotch, a cold sneer on his face and with eyes searing into me. Rising with zombie-like elegance, he gets to his feet. I gather by the curses he's mumbling under his breath that if he gets hold of me, I won't make it out of there alive. So I run—run, stagger, and half-fall all the way down the stairs and past the meth heads sleeping on the cement floor. I run, crying into the crystal-clear night, gasping breaths of cold air all the way to the overpass next to the busy highway on-ramp adjacent to the factory.

Guilt and fear swallow me. *Vulnerable, gullible, and stupid. That's you, you stupid twat—old Reggie was right and so were your instincts. Oh my God, Ultimate Being, I have to get to a phone—if I just leave them there, they'll be killed for sure.*

I run up the incline into the city to look for a pay phone, hoping that they still have those dinosaurs around for losers and homeless people, like me. My breath is fire in my throat by the time I spot one outside a take-out donair place. Coughing like an old smoker, I pick up the receiver and punch in 911. There's a short ring and a click.

"This is 911. What is your emergency?" a clear voice asks on the other end of the line.

I shout into the receiver. "My friends are in a factory with a bunch of stoned, drunk guys, and they're gonna get killed— they're being raped right now! Help them!"

"Okay, miss, stay calm—are you at the location now?"

"No, I got away—please send help—"

"Can you tell me where it is so I can dispatch help?" interrupts the calm operator.

"Uh. I think it was near the highway on-ramp off of—" I glance at the street sign on the corner. My vision is still swimming in front of me from the booze and pot, but I can make it out. "—Eastern Avenue! Please, hurry," I sob into the phone.

"The police and EMS are on the way to the factory location. What is your name, miss?"

"I'm—" I halt in mid-sentence and remember hearing somewhere that they trace 911 calls. They were probably tracing this one. I sure as hell don't want to be found, not drunk and stoned, with my shirt half-torn off. I'll end up in custody for sure, and eventually they'll send me home. I stare into the phone, then I hang up and run onto a side street, duck into an alley by a dumpster, and wait. I beg the Ultimate Being to help Taylor and Shaylee hang on until the police arrive.

Before long I hear the sound of sirens cut through the night air, *one, two, three*, one after the other, as they race down the busy street to the old factory district.

As I sit against the dumpster, I look down and wonder what to do about my torn-open shirt. I'm cold and my teeth are chattering and my face is streaked with tears, so I reach into my backpack side pocket to find a hoodie and something to wipe my face with. I dig around, and amongst a toothbrush, brush, and some change, I find a folded piece of paper. I open it up and it's the address Emma gave me so long ago in the Triple-S House. It's all in caps.

BRIAN—2145 QUEEN ST. E. 289 555 7722

# Chapter 20

I woke up the next morning in an alcove next to a bank machine, lying prone, with my head on my backpack. My thoughts rushed back to Taylor and Shaylee. *Shit, I hope the cops got to them before those animals could hurt them too badly. Did I make it to the phone in time?*

My stomach growled its hunger and I had to pee. I pulled my hood over my head for more warmth, and as I stumbled to my feet, a piece of paper fell out of my hand—the paper with Brian's address.

I bent over to pick it up, and the tears came again. I wondered if Emma was right about Brian. I turned the wrinkled slip of paper over in my hand. Hunger relentlessly bit my insides, but I was so tired—my legs hurt too much from running last night, so I let myself slide down to the floor again—at least it was warmer in the alcove.

I sat there, my arms wrapped around my knees, looking out onto the street. The hard shell I had worked so hard to build up over these months had shattered and fallen down around me. People filtered onto the street, the workers, the runners, the cyclists, and the dog walkers, all out for another day in the city, scurrying to work or to get their kids to school. I felt their eyes on me, judging me, their stares weighing me down until I couldn't breathe. I brushed the tears away and studied the paper again. My next thought, *Do I have anything to lose?*

"I need to have something to do today." The words were plain and simple but true. If I didn't focus on a task, I would lose it completely and go crazy right there on one of the busiest streets in Toronto.

So I stood up and strode out, feeling more fragile than I had ever felt, to panhandle for streetcar fare. I knew where that portion of Queen Street was—close to the Beaches. I found an empty paper cup in a garbage can, and began to beg.

Before long, I had enough to eat and take a streetcar. I went to a nearby coffee shop and ordered a hot chocolate and a doughnut. Nothing ever tasted so good. I peed, brushed my teeth, and washed in the bathroom. After that I walked to the streetcar stop and waited.

Queen Street is a damn long street. I watched the numbers on the buildings and houses flicker by as I rode the streetcar—1977, 1995, 2013. There were nice homes mixed with shops mixed with restaurants—not the place I would have expected the friend of a kid in a shelter to live.

There's 2087, 2117; it was close now, 2123. I pushed the

buzzer and got off. There weren't houses around, only stores. I walked to 2145, Mimi's Natural Grocer. Maybe Emma got the address wrong.

• • •

When I walk in, the clerk allows me a brief glance, then turns her attention back to cleaning the countertop. I probably look like a lost dog.

"Excuse me," I say softly. "I'm looking for this address." I show her the wrinkled and worn piece of paper.

She twists her head to look at it and smiles. "Yeah, Brian— he lives upstairs." She looks squarely at me now. "Go out and turn to your left—the white door right next to the display window. Let yourself in and go upstairs. It's Saturday, so he should be home."

I feel a little uplifted. "Thanks." I leave the store and do as I'm told. Left, then to the white door. It's open, just like she knew it would be. A narrow set of stairs rises in front of me, dark and smelling of mold. The carpet covering the worn, creaky steps hasn't seen a vacuum in years. I walk up gingerly and see two doors for, I'm guessing, two apartments. One door has "E. Lieberman" on it, the other "B. Elias"—I knock on B.'s door. Nothing. Knock again, harder.

"What!" A muffled shout, half-drowned out by the TV, comes from the other side. My heart jumps. What the hell am I going to say to this guy? *Is Emma home?*

"Are you Brian?" I wince.

"Who wants to know?" The voice is closer, but the TV still blares in the background.

"I'm Faith…I'm a friend of Emma's. We met at a shelter and she—" The door wrenches open wide. A slim man probably in his late twenties locks on to my eyes.

"How do you know Emma?"

Startled, I take a step back and stutter my response. "I—we met at a shelter."

"When!" He takes a step toward me. "When did you meet her! When's the last time you saw her?"

I back up to the wall.

"Have you seen her since—in the last couple months?"

"No, I haven't." My voice is small. He steps back into the apartment as he runs his hands through his hair, circles around a beat-up coffee table a few times, and flops down on a couch. Unsure of what to do, I return to the doorway and watch him warily as he hunches over and stares at the floor.

The man has a thin, pointed face, with buzz-cut hair, a scruffy beard, and a dagger tattoo on his forearm. I gather up the courage to ask again, only because I have nowhere else to go.

"Are you Brian?"

He nods slowly. "Yeah, I'm Brian."

"Um. Emma gave me this." I hold out the paper and cross the room to show him.

"She gave you that?" He lifts his eyes from the floor and grasps the paper.

I nod. "She said you guys were good friends, and she said that if I needed to, that I could stay with you and her."

"Well, Emma's been gone since July, so I guess you won't be seeing her." His voice is low and sad.

"Did you fight or something?" I ask cautiously.

"No, that's the thing—I don't know what happened. She just didn't come back."

"Where did she go?"

He looks at me pointedly. "Who are you anyway? And get back outside."

I turn and do as I'm told. "My name is Faith," I say from beyond the threshold.

"I know but…" He runs his fingers through his hair again. "What do you want? I told you, she's not here."

"Please…I just need someplace to sleep."

"Look," Brian says, getting up off the couch. "I can't just let you in here. You're obviously a kid. Don't you have a home? Parents?"

"I'm not from Toronto—and no, I don't," I lie. Just then, I hear a soft click as the other door opens. I turn my head slightly to see curious eyes looking at me from a crack in the door.

"What about a shelter?" he asks.

"I don't need a shelter, I need a job. I need to get a job so I can get my own place and start my life. If I go back to a shelter, I won't get a job—No one will hire me." My hands are palms up, in a desperate appeal. "I just need a chance, one chance. Please."

"So, like, you show up here…" His voice has a sarcastic drawl that angers me. I can feel my chest begin to heave. "And you expect me to let you sleep here and find you a job? Who the hell do you think you are?"

The door next to Brian's opens up a bit more, revealing a little old woman no taller than the chain lock securing her door. She looks ancient.

"I can't help you, so you need to leave." With this, he closes the door just as abruptly as he opened it; the breeze from the impact makes my hair fly back.

"Emma said you were a nice guy," I shout back to him. "She said you had a heart, but you're just a shit just like the rest of them." I swipe a tear from my cheek. "Sorry to bother you." I turn on my heel and begin to descend the stairs. I am nearly halfway down when I hear a woman's voice shout down to me.

"Stop, girlie." I halt in mid step. The old woman is at the top of the stairs, looking down at me. She's holding on to one of those rolling walkers, her forehead in a furrowed bunch and her eyes squinting at me, looking as though she was trying to make up her mind about me, weighing me. "How old are you?"

"I'm sixteen, Miss." There is something about her that commands respect.

"Sixteen." She shakes her head and breathes in deeply. "Where is Mama?" Her question pierces my heart.

"My momma is dead," I answer. The air hangs heavily between us.

After a long moment, she tells me, "You come up." Her accent is thick. "One night, one shower—then you go." I bob my head up and down, swallow hard, and feel immense pressure lifting from my chest. It's all I can do to not throw my arms around her and smother her with thank-yous. "Come, girlie." She motions for me to follow. "And if you steal anything, I call police."

I nod yes, staying a respectable distance behind her. "I

promise I won't. I know how that feels and I would never do it to anyone else." I follow her to her apartment and take my shoes off outside, shortly after which I notice that my socks aren't much cleaner than my shoes. She halts in the middle of her living room, which looks like it was trapped in the 1970s, and starts to say something, but the TV is blaring out a special report on the local news and both our eyes are drawn to the screen.

*"Police were called to an abandoned factory early this morning by an anonymous caller,"* says the female news anchor, *"where they discovered two female youths sexually assaulted and beaten unconscious. The females are now in hospital, where police say they are recovering from their injuries. In the meantime, six male youths ranging from fifteen to seventeen years of age and one man nineteen years of age are in custody. More to follow on this story as details become available."*

Taylor and Shaylee are alive. I bury my face in my hands and sob. I saved them. I saved them from those animals, who value the life and sexuality of a girl less than they do a piece of meat.

"What's wrong?" asks the old woman. It takes me a moment to catch my breath.

I shake my head, and my eyes are downcast. "Nothing," I say, though I want to cry out, *I know those girls and I called the police!*

As I try to steady my voice and choke down the next sob, I figure I had better introduce myself and thank her for letting me in. I'm not sure I would have done the same if I were in her shoes. "I'm sorry—I've had a rough couple of days. My name is Faith." I hold out my hand to shake. She looks at it—it's filthy. I retract it to save her the embarrassment of not taking it.

"My name is Edith Lieberman." She leans on her walker and continues to survey me up and down with wary eyes. "You call me Mrs. Lieberman."

"Nice to meet you, Mrs. Lieberman." I sniff and look around the apartment. It doesn't even look like it belongs in the same building as Brian's. It's warm and cozy, with embroidered doilies over all the upholstery armrests. The furniture is from another era, but it's clean and neat.

"You too," says Mrs. Lieberman. "You hungry?" Now that she mentions it, now that I know Taylor and Shaylee survived last night, I'm famished and I smell something cooking.

"Yes, I am. Very."

She shuffles to the rear of the apartment to a tiny galley kitchen. "I know it—you're too skinny. You like chicken?" she asks, serious and unsmiling.

I could eat a shoe. "I love chicken," I answer, my mouth watering. I follow her to the kitchen, where she picks up a wooden spoon and stirs a steaming pot. The aroma is mesmerizing.

"Good. Chicken with matzo balls—you like?" She turns and looks at me again, then shakes her head, which, in turn, makes me look down at myself.

"You go wash—go." She motions to a door opposite the kitchen. "You need clothes?"

"No, I have extra clothes in my bag."

She raises her brows. "They clean?" Her lips press together. "They not clean, you don't stay here."

"Well, not really all that clean." The ones I am wearing are my last clean change.

She looks under the kitchen sink and finds a bag. "Put clothes in there. Tomorrow, you bring to laundry." She's small in stature but definitely has a mind of her own.

"What do I wear instead?"

"My granddaughter's clothes—I get for you." Mrs. Lieberman shuffles into her bedroom and comes back with a handful of clothes on her walker seat: comfy-looking pyjamas, tidy whities, and socks. "My granddaughter was maybe your size—tall, like her father. My son."

"Mrs. Lieberman—I'm sorry—did she pass away?"

"What! Silly girl. She is now in university no—bigger—you are skinny and small."

"Oh, I'm sorry—I thought…never mind. Thank you." She's letting me use her granddaughter's clothes, allowing me to shower in her bathroom and she's feeding me—and she's letting me stay overnight. *Why would she show me such compassion*, I wonder—a street kid she doesn't know from any old scam artist?

I shrug and accept the kindness anyway. I take the bundle of clean clothes and the plastic bag.

"Use soap and shampoo—lots. Towels in cupboard." The corner of her mouth curls up just slightly into a smile, and her eyes betray an innate kindness, despite her brusque instructions.

At that point, I think she's the coolest. I nod yes and glide by the pot of chicken soup, simmering on the stove.

After my shower, I make certain that I clean up properly after myself and leave the bathroom in immaculate condition. Clean and freshly changed, bag of old clothes in hand, and ready to have a good meal, I feel like a new person.

"Come, girlie," says Mrs. Lieberman. "Soup is get cold." Balancing two glasses on her walker—one filled with milk, the other water—she shuffles over and places them on the table next to the steaming, hot bowls. I drop the bag at the door alongside my backpack and hurry to the table, reminding myself halfway there that this indulgence is only for one night.

As I sit down, I look at the spread in front of me, incapable of remembering such a healthy meal. Shelter food is okay, but this is in another category altogether. Chunks of carrots and celery swim around my big bowl of chicken soup, bumping up against the giant round dumplings, and on the side is a dish of what looks like pierogies, complemented by an overflowing breadbasket to my left.

I inhale deeply as I reach for my spoon. I barely touch it to my lips when she puts her hand out in front of me.

"Stop, girlie. Now we pray." She looks at me sternly, saying it as if I should have known all along that this was a necessary precursor to dinner, so I gingerly set my spoon down and bow my head. She takes a bowl from the side of the table and pours water over her hands, into another bowl, and says something in a language I've never heard.

I wait for it to be over, and take my host's lead, only taking up my spoon again when she does. I wait a few moments, just in case, then she finally says "Eat, girlie—what you waiting for?" like I should have known this, too.

I spoon soup into my mouth at lightning speed, relishing every bite of savory goodness. While doing so, I notice her looking at me and chortling softly.

"Mrs. Lieberman, the soup tastes delicious."

She nods as she slurps down a spoonful. "Thank you. Is matzo ball soup," she says as she points to my plate.

"Oh." I watch as she takes a pierogi and bites into it.

"Try one," she says, shoving the side dish closer.

"Sure," I say. "I love pierogies."

She shakes her head. "No," she says flatly. "This is knish. Is Jewish."

"Okay…. Are you Jewish, Mrs. Lieberman?"

My host glances at me for a moment, raises her brows, and laughs softly. "Matzo ball soup, knishes, and Lieberman—yes, Jewish." She chortles out loud now, a little harder, and I can't help joining her—her laughter is infectious.

"I don't know any Jewish people. There aren't many where I come from," I say.

"Too bad for you," she remarks matter-of-factly. I have to laugh at that.

"You Catholic?"

"No."

"Protestant?"

"Um—not really. I'm not anything." I look down, embarrassed that I'm not anything. I stick my fork in one of the knishes and bite into it. An explosion of rich, savory flavor bursts in my mouth. I'm beginning to feel sleepy from a full stomach and not enough sleep the night before.

"Where is family?" blurts out Mrs. Lieberman, taking me by surprise.

"I told you, I don't have one."

"I don't believe." I sense that her eyes are fixed on me, figuring me out. I shake my head and rub my eyes.

"Fine," she inhales deeply, standing to stack the dishes. "You finish, then you sleep." The old woman sets the plates on her walker seat and rolls them into the kitchen. My need for sleep is winning the battle over my curiosity about Mrs. Lieberman. Why is she being good to me? I will ask her before I leave tomorrow. For now, I have to set my head down and close my eyes.

"Sofa is comfortable. There is blanket and pillow in closet. You sleep now." I'm not about to argue with her.

# Chapter 21

I try to get to Taylor, but strong hands are holding me back. She and Shaylee are crying, bleeding, gasping. Strong hands are holding them down, too. I can't breathe; I open my mouth wide to scream, but nothing comes. I feel a hand shaking my shoulder, and I try to reach to pry it off, but my arm may as well be made of stone. I open my eyes and see the outline of a little old woman and light from a window flooding the apartment behind her.

"Mrs. Lieberman?" I croak.

"Yes, girlie." She looks kindly at me. "You cry in sleep."

As I rub the sleep from my eyes, I look around the place. Yep, I was still here, no abandoned factory, no Taylor, and no Shaylee—just me. "I was having a nightmare."

Mrs. Lieberman grunts her agreement. "You call someone in sleep. You call family, yes?"

I shake my head no and think for a moment about not telling her, then I don't think anymore. "The two girls on the news last night—the ones the police found—they were my friends." I see her mind working, then finally it clicks.

She puts a hand to her mouth. "They in hospital?" she asks.

I nod. "They were beaten by boys who drugged us—I was there, too, but I got away. I don't know how I got away, but I called the police and they got there in time. I thank the Ultimate Being for that." Mrs. Lieberman mumbles something in another language as she clutches her chest.

"Who is this Ultimate Being?"

I shrug. "God, I guess."

She smiles. "You and friends stay out of trouble—then no need for HaShem to save you. Come to breakfast."

"Um. What time is it, Mrs. Lieberman?"

"Nine. You sleep sixteen hours. Must be very tired." She appears from the galley kitchen with more crockery on her walker seat. A bowl full of piping hot oatmeal smelling like cinnamon and apples, along with a giant mug of steaming hot milk. She places the bowl and mug at the same spot where I sat last night.

"You made that for me?" I feel spoiled—a feeling that has been foreign to me for most of my life.

"Yes. Come!" Her voice is jokingly impatient, so I smile and obey. Her little body turns back into the kitchen and returns with a cup of tea. She places it on the table, then sits down, and watches with pleasure as I eat.

"Thank you so much for feeding me." I wipe my mouth and look at her with what I hope is appreciation. "How can I ever repay you, Mrs. Lieberman? You saved my life last night. I don't know what I would have—"

"Shh!" She puts a finger to her lips. "Enough, girlie." She gathers up the plates and hobbles to the kitchen again, putting them in the sink. Then she turns and reaches up, feeling for something on top of her fridge. She comes back with a change purse tucked in her palm and hands it to me. "Take money— you go to laundry and wash clothes. I make grocery list for you, and you shop for me. You help old woman, I help young girl. You stay another day—yes?" She looks at me with sweet eyes that are trying hard to be stern. My own eyes sting with tears despite my best efforts to hold them back.

"Okay," I whisper. "Yeah, I can do that for you." She's throwing me a lifeline and she knows it, but doesn't want to compromise my dignity.

I stay that day. I wear her granddaughter's clothes to the Laundromat, I do her groceries while my clothes wash and dry, then go back to her place with her food. She makes me dinner and I sleep on the couch again. The next day, she gives me money for clothes. As I walk out, I see Brian unlocking his door.

"What are you doing here?" he asks, taken by surprise.

"Mrs. Lieberman asked me to stay," I mumble as I look down and walk past him.

"You better not be ripping her off, or stealing from her. She's a nice lady. And she's been through enough."

"I'm not." I sneer at him. "And I know she's nice. She

helped me, unlike someone else." I make my eyes look hard and narrow them to slits. Then I continue to descend the steps and exit through the door next to the grocer.

I find a secondhand store—they call it vintage. I pick up some pants and sweaters. I'm in heaven. Safe, cared for, clean, and fed, appreciating small kindnesses like I never have before. I go back and we watch TV, talk, and eat together.

The next day, I help Mrs. Lieberman down the stairs and we go for frozen yogurt. Everyone in the shop knows her, like she's a celebrity. Then we go back up to her apartment, where she announces that she wants to teach me how to make knishes. This is an entire afternoon. We make the filling and are about to roll out the dough when she asks me the question again.

"Girlie," she says, "Who is your family?" I wince at the question because, even though I lie like an expert, I know that I can't lie to her. She'll know if I do. "You have mama, papa? Brother, sister? You don't believe, but is true—they worry."

I don't answer her question. I'm too afraid to tell her, in case her intention is to call someone to come get me "for my own good." Then the police would show up and drag me back to that hellhole neighborhood in Greenleigh—back to counselors and therapists with endless stupid questions. And back to my grandmother, that sour old prune who drove my mom away. And to Constance, who's ashamed of me and my low-life ways. *No thanks, Mrs. Lieberman, I'm staying here as long as you'll let me, thank you very much.*

In the end, Mrs. Lieberman lets it drop and keeps on working.

"These will be good," she says, taking pride in her handiwork. "Very good."

"Where did you learn how to make knishes, Mrs. Lieberman?"

"My mama teach me," she answers as she cleans the table, her mind clearly focused on the task at hand.

"That's nice—my mother never taught me anything."

Mrs. Lieberman's eyes lock on to mine. "So you do have mama." She thinks she has me.

"*Had.* She died a couple years ago from septicemia. My mother was an IV drug user—she got an infection from dirty needles and never got better. She was too weak to fight it off."

Mrs. Lieberman stands beside me and listens. "I am sorry." Her voice is soft, and laced with sadness. She pats my shoulder, then shakes her head and takes the cloth to the sink to rinse it.

"Yeah, me too."

"Is why you run away?" asks Mrs. Lieberman.

"Partly. But there were other reasons that had nothing to do with my mother. It's a whole bunch of reasons."

She turns to me, the twinkle in her eye now gone. "Father beat you?"

"No—I don't really know him."

"You live at foster's home?"

"With my grandmother, but she…she's not really like a grandmother. She's…cold."

Mrs. Lieberman raises a brow. "Only you and grandma?"

"I have two sisters. One younger, one older. The older one I thought was my best friend—but when I found out she's actually embarrassed to be related to me, I couldn't take it anymore."

My story spills out of me like I've pulled off a giant scab and my words are bleeding uncontrollably all over the kitchen counter. Mrs. Lieberman sits on one of her dining room chairs, and listens.

I admit to her that I always felt out of place at school, the oddball, moody, miserable kid. I tell her that I was centered out because of my family situation, about the embarrassment of being bullied—and that I decided to fulfill my portended role as a dirty, unkempt, crazy, angry mess because people said that's what I was most of my life. I tell her how lost and abandoned I felt when my mother would leave us, how I thought she was the only one who knew me and could save me. And then how I felt we were never enough for her, and how frustrated I was with her, deep down (though I had never admitted it to anyone because that would've meant my mother was at fault). And about how angry I was that I was left with my Gran and had to look after both me and Des because, according to Gran, she had already raised her kid and wasn't about to raise her daughter's kids, too. Mrs. Lieberman flinched at that one.

I tell her that I was upset with Connie 'cause she left and got to live with Josie. Then, of course, there was my friendship with Norma and Ishaan, two misfits who were as willing as I was to experiment with any available substance to get away from their realities. I admit that the experiments increased when the reality of my mother's death hit home at a formative time in my life, when I needed her guidance and loving hand the most. Then I tell her about the whole nineteenth birthday party fiasco, my run, and the last nine months or so on the street, culminating with the factory party disaster, which almost got me killed. Of course, the story wouldn't be complete without telling Mrs. Lieberman about Emma, who is now missing, and her suggestion to come see Brian, which led me to this kindly old woman in the first place. I finish with a deep breath and shrug, and wait for a response.

I expect to hear something like "Poor girlie, you so hard done by—you have such hard life"—anything. Instead, she remains silent.

Mrs. Lieberman purses her lips tightly and digests the information spewed at her by this runaway she's taken in. I'm certain she's rethinking her choice, but then she takes my hand and orders me to make us a fresh pot of tea.

"Nice and strong—then I tell you my story."

• • •

I listen, drinking my tea, as Mrs. Lieberman recounts with chilling detail the horrific story of her childhood, about Poland and the Second World War when Hitler and his Nazis tried to eliminate all of Europe's Jews. She tells me about her once happy early life and how the war changed her formative years so horribly—how her parents were separated, and how her mother hid her only beloved child in the trunk of a car and paid someone to smuggle her out of Warsaw and into Hungary. She remembers not wanting to say good-bye and how she never saw her parents again; she found out later that they had been murdered in Treblinka.

Mrs. Lieberman tells me about ghettos and camps, disease and starvation, exhausting treks across mountains, and her eventual rescue when she was hidden among Christian children in an orphanage. She tells me about the terror, the torture, the unfathomable death toll on her people—about the inhumanity ordinary people are capable of. Her tears flow freely. So do mine. She sniffs and then her gaze falls on me.

"I'm so sorry, Mrs. Lieberman," is all I can think of to say.

"I sorry too. I survive, yet my mama and papa were killed like dogs." Years of guilt and sadness are etched on her face.

"But you were a little girl, Mrs. Lieberman. You couldn't have done anything."

The old woman draws in a shuddering breath, then grasping my teacup along with hers, she places them on her walker and heads to the kitchen.

"Anyway, that is how I survive. Mama—she brave and strong. She save me."

I move to the kitchen, too. "That's just it, Mrs. Lieberman. I don't have a brave, strong mother to rescue me. I have no one."

Mrs. Lieberman turns to me. "Then *you* must have courage. *You* save you. Promise, girlie. Go home, find family, make peace." The urgency in her voice is clear, her worries about me are evident, though I'll never know why she gave me a second thought.

• • •

That night as I lay on her couch, watching the streetlights reflected on her ceiling, I couldn't get the images of Mrs.

Lieberman's story out of my mind. Maybe Mrs. Lieberman *was* destined to save someone. I thought, *What if that someone is me?*

Sleep finally rolled around and took me over, but unsettling images shook me awake a few times that night, resulting in a wild bed-head and red eyes the next morning—a small sacrifice for learning Mrs. Lieberman's terrible, awful, moving truth. Yes, she was damaged—who wouldn't be. But she had managed to turn a page and live her life. She'd come to Canada, gotten married, had a son, had a granddaughter. She inspired me and gave me hope that I just might be able to do as she asked; to go home and make peace, so *I* could have peace. This little old woman had more strength and grit in her thumbnail than I had in my entire body.

# Chapter 22

I stayed with Mrs. Lieberman for another week. She taught me to cook and talked to me all the time. She told me about her son, Noam, who lived in Montreal and was an investment banker. She said he wanted her to move there to be closer to him, but she wouldn't. Her husband had chosen Toronto, and she would stay here. Noam also wanted to move her to another apartment, a newer condo in a better neighborhood, but she was accustomed to her street and knew where everything was— she was afraid she would get lost in a new neighborhood. I went to sleep that night thinking I was the luckiest person on Earth to have found my rescuer in such a kindly, gentle old woman.

...

On the third Thursday after Mrs. Lieberman first invited me to stay, I wake up as usual. After I shower, I make coffee. It's unusual for her to sleep beyond seven. I know this because she always manages to wake me with her kitchen bustling. At eight, I begin wondering if she couldn't sleep the night before and is sleeping in. By nine, I'm getting worried. I step softly to her bedroom door, knock the obligatory three times. No answer. Again, I knock, louder this time.

I open the door, just a crack, and peek in. She's lying on her side, facing away from me. I feel an ominous foreboding wrap around me. Her blanket isn't moving in the up-and-down rhythmic way a blanket does when the person underneath is breathing. I step around the bed and move her walker over so I can get to her. Mrs. Lieberman's face is bluish and blotchy. Panic starts rising in my throat. I reach out with a shaking hand to gently caress hers, which is still holding on to the edge of her fleece blanket. It's ice cold.

I back away, struggling to breathe because every last molecule of oxygen has left my lungs and I'm startled and dis-oriented, trying to remember what to do.

*Help. Ambulance.*

I stumble to the wall phone and call 911. I'm crying to the lady on the other end, that Mrs. Lieberman went to bed the night before and never woke up this morning. She asks for Mrs. Lieberman's address and then asks a few questions, and then she says to stay there until the police and first responders come. After I hang up, I go to her bedroom door and close it—I just figure it's the right thing to do—to give her the dignity of privacy for the last time.

Dazed, I look around and find a slim green address book

on a table next to the phone, with a picture of ivy on it, and inside there's a 1996 calendar in the beginning pages. The pages are all yellow and dog-eared. I look for her son's phone number under the *L*s but I find it under the *N*s—Noam Lieberman. I should be the one to tell him, not some cold policeman or doctor, that his mother just passed. I was with her last, so I owe her that much.

After I dial his number, I get his voicemail. It says the usual thing, so I leave a message. Though I want to tell him in person, I don't know how long I'll have access to a phone—I can't stay here any longer.

I get my backpack near the door, quickly put the rest of my stuff in it, and leave. As I'm exiting the door next to the grocer, the first responders are just arriving and unloading their gurney from the back of the ambulance. A fire truck is right behind them, and a police car is coming from the opposite end of the street. As I pass nearby stores with my hoodie on over my head, my coat buttoned, and my backpack slung over my shoulder, people are coming out to see what all the commotion is about.

I take a last look at Mrs. Lieberman's window on the second floor. Her plants, green and healthy, sitting on the window ledge soaking in the uncharacteristically bright November sun, are unaware that, in a short time, they will shrivel and die because no one will be there to water them. I feel grief and sadness for my loss of one of a few people on Earth who accepted me for who I was.

As tears begin to flow I wonder why the people I cared about are always leaving me.

# Chapter 23

I walk and walk in the cold sunlight. Tears are rising up in my eyes again, but there are too many people on the sidewalk to let go, so I duck into an alley behind some big blue recycling bins and weep. It was nice to be someone to somebody for a while, but now that is over. My tears ebb and flow as I think of her blue eyes, cloudy with cataracts, yet still brilliant with life. I hear broken English as she scolds me when I ruin the blintze dough. "Oy, girlie, why you no listen!" She pretends to be pissed, but she really isn't.

*She gave me the keys so I could unlock my own truths.*

I promised Mrs. Lieberman I would do it, so I will. She allowed me a glimpse into her life so I could fix mine.

Maybe I'll do it. Maybe I'll try.

I get up again and walk, walk, walk around. I go nowhere but I walk for hours.

• • •

A loud crash, then a thud reverberates in my head and I jump with a start. I open my eyes, and there's a man with an empty plastic bin in his hands, looking down at me. My head is resting against a dumpster.

"You can't stay here—restaurant's opening soon."

I say, "Okay." No emotion, no anger or shame.

My mouth feels parched and my stomach hurts for food. I consider panhandling, then decide not to—maybe the first responders left the door open to Mrs. Lieberman's and I can go in and get some milk and latkes. My heart aches when I think of her, cold and lifeless, when only a short time ago, she gave me more hope for a life than ever.

I will my feet to move and head back to Mrs. Lieberman's apartment. Everything looks quiet, so I go in the white door at the side of the grocer. I walk up the stairs and stop at the top step, looking at Mrs. Lieberman's door. I hear people inside, and figure it's her family.

I step closer. I want to knock and say I knew her and she was awesome, but Brian's door opens instead.

"Hey! It's you again," says Brian—he's got overalls on.

I look at the floor and keep silent. He's probably thinking that I had something to do with her death, that I stressed her out and gave her a heart attack or something.

"I heard she died, in her sleep, right?" he says softly.

I nod, my eyes still on the floor. "I found her yesterday morning—called 911."

"You okay?" he asks. I shrug and look at him for a split second and keep silent. My eyes are welling up but I'm keeping it together.

"Look, I feel like shit, the way I treated you. I was in a pretty bad space, ya know?" He shifts his weight from one foot to the other. "You sleep on the street last night?" My gaze meets his again as I nod yes, and he breathes hard and rolls his eyes a little.

"I gotta go to work. You wanna come in? Have something to eat maybe." He waits for a response.

I say, "Okay."

I go into his apartment, and he points out the fridge and the couch. Then he says, "I gotta go. If you leave before I get back and you've stolen my shit, I'll find you and kick your ass."

I feel better when he leaves. I put down my backpack and find some bread and peanut butter and jam and make a sandwich and pour myself a glass of milk. Then I turn on the TV and watch talk shows, crying like a two year old and eventually fall asleep on the couch.

I'm comatose until I hear the door open. My senses come to life, and I look around, orienting myself.

"Did you sleep?" I hear a voice from the other side of the alcove.

"Uh, yeah," I say, shaking my head. I look for the time and find it on the digital clock on the stove. It's five o'clock and already dusk outside. "Thanks for, uh…letting me stay." I rub the sleep from my eyes. He comes into the room with a pizza in his hand. "I hardly got any sleep last night—it was kind of cold and I didn't have a heavy coat. Or…a sleeping bag or anything…." My mind is still working on being awake and connecting to my speech center.

"Got some pizza. Hungry?" he says.

"Yeah." We eat in silence. I keep thinking of what Mrs. Lieberman made me promise. So I wipe my mouth after the second slice and I ask if I can use his phone.

"I want to try to go home. This may sound weird, but Mrs. Lieberman kind of made me promise to at least try. It's been awhile, but I think a good place to start would be to call my Gran." He sits there, with a half-eaten slice of pizza in his hand, blinking at me. "Can I use your phone?"

"Sure. Do you want them to know where you are?" He takes a flip phone from a drawer in the coffee table and hands it to me. "If you don't want them to, this is the phone to use. I hope it works out for you—honest, I do."

I take it, but my hand is shaking. "It's to Greenleigh, so it's long distance," I say.

"No worries." He motions with his head to the phone. "Just call."

I'm so nervous to do it, but my hand grasps the old Nokia and I punch in Gran's phone number. All these months she hasn't heard from me, and here I am calling right out of the blue.

It rings three times and then someone picks up. "Hello?" It's Des.

I take in a deep breath. "Hi, Des. It's Faith." I hear a gasp. Inside I'm trembling.

"Faith?" she says, her voice barely over a whisper. Then, more urgently, "Did you say it's Faith?"

"Yeah, Des. I'm okay." I cover my eyes so Brian can't see me blubbering like a baby. "It's me, Faith, and I'm okay."

A strangled cry and sobs pierce my eardrum. "Where are you? Oh my God, Faith, where are you? We thought you were dead. We went to the police and all that, but…nothing. Where are you?"

"Don't worry, I'm okay. I was on the street, but then I stayed with this amazing, little old lady, and she really helped me see things—"

I hear muffled shouts on the other end, then sounds of the phone changing hands.

"Faith, goddamn it—is that you?" Gran. "Do you have any fucking idea what you put everyone through?"

My breathing escalates and becomes shallow. I bolt up from the couch and start to pace. "Yeah—I'm sorry, Gran, but something happened, and I couldn't stay there anymore—I needed to get away."

Gran shouting. "Yeah, I know what happened all right—"

Des screaming. "Gran! Stop! What are you—"

Me crying. "If I didn't get away, I think I would have hurt myself, Gran—I'm sorry! But—!"

Gran shouting. "Don't 'sorry' me! What the hell were you thinking?"

Me. "I'm trying to tell you. I ran away 'cause I heard Connie say something really bad, and on top of all the other stuff going on in my head, I thought I was gonna—"

Gran, with fresh anger. "Yeah, that's another thing! Connie said you ran off with one of her friend's coats and a shitload of money—"

Des. "Shut up, Gran—gimme the phone, she's gonna hang up—" Shuffling and something breaking. I picture the cheap pink glass vase in the kitchen toppling over the countertop in the Lego house in Greenleigh.

Gran. "Are you taking drugs now, too, wherever you are?" I'm pacing and Brian's watching. "Don't you know your mother died 'cause of drugs?"

Me. "No, Gran—Mom died 'cause she had mental health issues. She died 'cause her husband died and she couldn't handle it." Then I spit out a last comment that I've been wanting to say to her since I was able to see things as they really are. "She died 'cause of *you!* 'Cause you're a mean old bitch. You drove her away and made her feel like shit, just like you make me feel like shit! Put Destiny back on the phone!"

I hear her curse and then the sounds of the phone changing hands again.

"Faith, don't listen to her. You know how she is—she wants you home—"

"I can't take her anymore, Destiny! I'm not like you. I'm like Mom, and if I come back, I'll either kill her or I'll kill myself." The words are hanging in the air between my sister and me, and I can see her as she tries to figure out how to undo the damage done by Gran.

"Faith, tell me where you are. I'll come get you myself."

I try to offer her some solace. "Don't worry about me, Des.

Promise. I'm fine." I press the hang-up button as she starts to talk again. My shaking hand passes the phone to Brian as I sit down on the couch and let my head hang back onto the faded upholstery.

What would Mrs. Lieberman have me do now? I screwed up again.

Brian shakes his head and opens up the back of the phone, takes the SIM card out, and shoots it in the ashtray. "Christ, your grandmother's a bitch." He breathes out hard through his nose. I stare at the ceiling and wipe my eyes with my hoodie sleeve. "Are you okay?" he asks.

"Would you be?"

"No. Probably not." We are quiet for a long time. Then he shrugs and pulls open the coffee table drawer again and takes out a joint and a lighter. "Do you wanna smoke? Looks like you could use it."

I look at the joint and the lighter. It's a textbook roll, tapered at both ends and faultlessly even.

"I think I will." My anger has turned to hard resentment. Why should I be good if no one believes me or appreciates how hard it is to stay good on the street. Gran's lucky I haven't turned to prostitution like a lot of the kids do. No—she has no idea how good I was.

Poor Destiny. Maybe I'll call her back tomorrow.

"Do you have anything—you know, stronger?" I hear myself ask.

"Hell yeah," he answers and rises to go to the bedroom.

# Chapter 24

It's heroin. Brian holds the cache in his hand like a pirate grasps plunder. He walks back into the living room with a plastic sack of powder that looks like sifted dirt. In his other hand he's got tinfoil, a lighter, and a small metal tube. A sober silence stretches between us as he lights the powder, which smells like burned barbecue sauce.

He teaches me how to chase the dragon, and soon I feel Darkness lifting. It slips away, pushed by a surge of gentle euphoria. A warm flush swells on my skin, a dry mouth, and heavy extremities—like I'm not strong enough to lift my own arm—but I don't want to. I just want to feel it; the calm and the peace, the stillness—even the nausea doesn't bother me. Sleepiness takes me next, and I go on the nod, an alternately wakeful and drowsy state.

I'm not sure if it's later that day or the day after, but Brian brings out another fold. His lips draw back as he takes in the smoke. After that, we do it again.

I hear people outside his door, hushed voices and footsteps, like ghosts floating in and out, but I don't react, 'cause they are in the apartment next door. I don't care anymore that Mrs. Lieberman has died and that no one else gives a shit about me, because I feel so relaxed and blissfully apathetic, wrapped up in my cozy little cotton ball of heroin.

Time is fluid, elegantly slipping in and out of my cup of indifference as the animal in my gut leaves me for a while and I touch peace.

It's like when people tell me that everything is going to be okay—this is what it's like; this is "okay."

I can't remember eating or drinking or peeing. I can't even remember if we have sex. Maybe it's only the heroin making me feel a gentle orgasm, the absence of fear and loneliness, plus a physical feeling in which all muscles relax. My entire body feels like it's being cradled in a giant, supple baseball glove, or like the feeling of getting into a cool, soft bed after having walked ten miles on thorns with a burning cross on my back.

I chase the dragon again, the white curly smoke.

Right now, my troubles seem far away, but what I don't know is, they are poised to get much worse.

# Chapter 25

I marvel at how fast it happened. How easily I got hooked. As easy as walking through a forest, enjoying the wonder of nature, and then stepping into the most jagged bear trap ever created. It snaps tight around you with lightning speed and squeezes you—not letting you die, but taking your life slowly and painfully while nature still abounds within reach.

Everything eventually gets quiet next door at Mrs. Lieberman's, and I guess the funeral is done. I feel guilty that I missed it, but only for a minute because Brian comes back from his brother's place and is looking really scared.

"Faith, you gotta get outta here," he says out of breath as he shuts the door and locks it.

"Why?" I'm feeling pretty lucid for having only smoked an a-bomb a couple hours ago.

"'Cause my brother's coming and he's a crazy fuck. He's pissed 'cause I've been using with you."

"So? What's he gonna do—kill me?" I smile at him, still a little floaty.

"Well, yeah—or maybe he'll just kick the shit out of you or beat you until you don't recognize yourself." I see sweat beads on his forehead. "I couldn't get any more H from him. He says he doesn't want me getting hooked, 'cause he's got enough junkies around him without having a brother for a freak, too."

I look at him and blink. Is he telling me to leave?

"So, you're throwing me out?"

"Jesus—you've been here almost two weeks and high the entire time. This might be a good time to…maybe you should go home."

"You heard what happened when I tried that…my Gran won't even—"

"You have to go!" He races around the apartment, gathers my stuff together, and crams everything into my backpack. "All you've done is get high—you need to go."

"Well, you gave it to me, asshole—you gave me the heroin!" I can't believe what I'm hearing. He's pissed because I'm doing what he wanted me to do. "Now you're mad 'cause I like it?"

"I gave it to you to help you get over a rough spot—not to get you hooked. And you asked for it—remember?" Brian looks panicked—I don't know if it's because he thinks he's gotten me hooked or because he's afraid of his brother. Maybe a little of both. "Look, I'll be honest. I went to Henry's to get more H today, and he asked what the hell I was doing 'cause he knows I only do it occasional-like. So I says to him that I have a friend staying with me and that you are having a rough time on account of your family and all, and then he blows up at me and says he won't sell me any more 'cause you're getting it for nothing when he should be selling it to you for street."

"And how much is that—like one hit?"

"Fifteen dollars."

"How many hits a day have I been chasing?"

"Five or six—sometimes up to eight."

"Holy shit—where am I gonna get that kind of money?"

"Hey, it's not my problem. All I did was help you out and bring you up." He thrusts the backpack at my stomach. "I can give you Henry's contact address. You gotta deal with him now."

Who the hell would have thought that when I came out of the nods this late afternoon, I would be thrown out of yet another two-week couch-surfing stretch. "Fine." I'm apathetic as hell. I can't feel anything and I don't care. "I'll go." I rummage through a side pocket of my backpack and find five dollars and sixty-five cents, which I pull out and hold up to him. "This is all I have. I'm going to need a hit soon." The words strike me between the eyes, battering my head and beating my soul. *I'm going to need a hit.* This is where I realize for the first time that I'm an addict—in two short cloudy, obscure weeks, my body has grown accustomed to the chemicals I've been putting in my lungs and is craving more.

Brian stuffs his hands into his pockets and pulls out two twenties and some loose change. "Take it. And here." He scoops up a rolling paper from the coffee table and scratches some numbers and a street name on it. "That's Henry's address—for more smack. Now go. I'm serious: He's on his way here. Don't tell him you're the one who's been sucking up all my brown sugar."

I nod listlessly. "I have to pee, then I'll go." With my backpack in hand, I shuffle to the bathroom and look in the mirror as I pull down my pants. Blank, waxy complexion, dark circles under my eyes, sunken cheeks, about ten pounds thinner, and greasy hair.

When I walk back out, he's holding up a roll of foil and a lighter. "You're gonna need these, too."

• • •

With continued use, I need increasing amounts of smack just to feel "normal." I did meet up with Henry, who knew that I was the one who had hooked up with Brian. He joked that I was the latest of Brian's pet projects, laughed that his brother picked up stray girls off the street like others pick up stray cats and dogs. "I guess he just can't help himself—sixty bucks. I'll let you have five for four."

"Thanks," I mumble with my eyes downcast. I turn away from his oily face and walk out of the rear door of the bar where we meet, into an alley.

I met him nearly a month ago at his house, which was about three blocks from Brian's place. I buy here now—they trust me.

It's late December. I walk and I see lights and Christmas

trees in storefronts and inside living rooms of the houses I pass to buy my next hit. Panhandling is a breeze right now, because people are feeling all warm and fuzzy and sentimental because it's the holidays. I try to ration my money in case I can't make enough tomorrow. I've been slow a few times in chasing up as I need more and more to feel like a human. I get irritable and edgy, restless. My muscles throb and my bones ache. I'm cold and my legs get jittery.

I wonder how many times Brian has done this—inadvertently drummed up customers for his brother—I feel like I was duped, tricked, and misled into believing Brian had given me smack to ease my pain, when all the while he was recruiting new customers for his brother. He can't fool me with this *you did it to yourself* act. Henry was probably happy I was using, not pissed like Brian said he was.

# Chapter 26

I was alone. Completely, totally, entirely alone. That place people wish they never journey to in their lives was where I was at.

It was March in Toronto, the sky, steel gray and cold—the coldest I could remember. I don't know why, but my mind kept drifting back to that crocus in Gran Dot's front yard. In a week or two, the crocus would sprout in the little patch of earth. I wanted to see it bloom, but Greenleigh was far away. I had no money, no friends, and no way to get there.

I had mixed feelings about Mom. I never wondered if her love for her kids was genuine, of that I was certain, but I was resentful that she wasn't there for me when I needed her. Connie had Josephine to love her and care for her, and I had no one. I suppose that the inequality of my sister's and my situation brought me to question why I was taking up space on this planet when most days, all I wanted to do was end the Darkness.

And now that was fading, too.

I wanted to do it so badly. I wanted to end the pain and push away the Darkness and demons that had been chasing me ever since I could remember. I wanted to feel nothing. Finish the cycle of disappointment. Float. Be free.

My struggle had ended, and I was content to finally come to realize it. That night, instead of sleeping in a store alcove or hiding my smoking stuff and heading for a shelter, I would stay on the street. Instead of shivering on a busy side street off of Yonge, I would find a quiet alley, sit down on a piece of newspaper, and fall asleep. I would rest. Then all the hurt would be gone. I could picture all my dirty, tattered clothes being replaced by flowing, white gossamer robes. I would smell fragrant gardens instead of exhaust and garbage, and I would feel peaceful and loved instead of hateful and neglected. No more couch surfing or stealing or begging for money to buy my next fix.

It was still dusk. Too early to hide in the alley. As I reasoned and planned my escape from this world, I stepped into an alcove. It was the entrance to the Bank of Montreal, the place where people go to the instant teller to get their money. I used to ask people for money there, but I figured it made them really uncomfortable, seeing as how it was right beside the bank machine and all, so I didn't anymore. I slid down the side of the glass wall inside the bank alcove, away from the gusty cold air, and waited. My lumpy knapsack, filled with everything I owned in the world, dug into my back as I sat there motionless, in pain but not caring.

I was so tired. Tired of figuring out where my next handful of change was coming from; what I would have to do to get enough money for my next hit; who I would have to steal from. I was tired of living only for the next fix, of structuring my life around the next hit, of watching other users on the street die or heal, and of me being stalled in the same place. I was emaciated and feeling filthy, inside and out. My clothes were dirty and tattered and way too big. I'd lost my way and my purpose. My soul was broken—I'd lost Faith. Lost hope. Lost my belief in my own destiny.

With those thoughts in mind, I tucked my legs in and wrapped my arms around them, to make sure no one tripped over me. It was best to wait till it got darker because I knew that if I went in the back alley too early, the light would give me away and I would be discovered by someone taking out the garbage from one of the businesses or restaurants on the street.

I sniffed up my runny nose and waited. People looked at me, some with disdain, some with pity, some with indifference. But none looked at me like I was human, if they looked at all. I occasionally got some change thrown my way.

"Give a man a fish, and he'll eat for a day. Teach a man to fish…" That adage came to mind and I thought about learning to fish, about the calmness of being on a lake somewhere up north in the summer, and fishing.

Thinking made me sleepy. I closed my eyes and let my forehead rest on my knees. I had the nods. But if I fell asleep here, someone would call the cops, so I had to stay awake. Since I had decided, I didn't want to take the chance of messing this up, too, and be taken to a shelter. I opened my eyes and moved my head to one side and looked at the people walking by, at the stoplight on the corner—red, amber, green, red, amber, green… repeat. Was Gran looking for me? Did anyone still wonder where I was, or had they given up searching for me? Had Gran even called the police and reported my last call?

My eyes were heavy and the light was now starting to fade. It would be dark in the back alley soon. I would find a place behind a dumpster and just fall asleep. The cold would do the rest. I would just sleep and never wake up. It would be painless and sweet.

But first, I needed to close my eyes just for a minute, to give them a rest and enjoy my last high. My eyelids fell heavily and everything went away. I was almost in a light sleep when a series of squeals and giggles startled me.

"Those dumb-ass girls," I mutter. They're chattery and loud. Passersby have no regard for the homeless. "Shut up," I mumble, and I turn my head to face away as I huff out an impatient breath. I want peace in my last moments of aloneness, here by the instant teller machine. As I sit in a grimy rumple on the floor of this doorway, I crave quiet and stillness in the midst of the disarray that has been my life.

Thank Christ! The chatter and laughter stop. But then it's replaced by a gasp and an almost inaudible "Oh my God."

It's a whisper. Only the sound of the breath over the tongue, the way the mouth shapes the vowels, and how the lips work to form the consonants—but I recognize it. The lilt of the whisper is unmistakable.

It's Constance.

I look up and make immediate eye contact. It is her, and she's flanked by two other girls whose boots cost more than I had collected in change all year.

She stands over me, taller and more womanly than I remember her. Her hair is longer, and lighter. I note that her braces are off as she opens her mouth and shapes it into a stunned smile.

"Faith! It is you!" Her hands fly to her mouth. Then, she impulsively reaches out. "Oh my God! You're alive! Where have you been?" I don't wait for her to reach me—I spring up in such a way that I surprise even myself.

"This is Faith?" says one of the girls with her.

"Your sister?" asks the other. My eyes dart from Constance to her friends and back to Constance. She still has her arms out waiting for me to fall into an embrace. I'm not sure if I should indulge her.

"Yeah, it's her sister, bitch," I say with a sneer. The two recoil. I guess they were expecting me to fall at Connie's feet or something like that. Constance continues to smile and unflinchingly holds out her arms to me.

"Faith…please. Come on." She takes a step toward me. I stick out my arm and shove her hands away.

"Don't you dare touch me," I hiss as I march past her and down the street to O'Keefe Lane, bumping violently into more than a few pedestrians as I rush by.

"Stop—Faith, wait!" Connie shouts after me. I hear her boots clicking on the pavement close behind me as I round the corner to get to the alleyway. My spot is just off O'Keefe behind Yonge Street—if I can only make it there, I can find a place to hide. I want her to go away—now that I have made the decision. It's taken me so long to work up the courage to finally do it, I don't want anyone taking my resolve away.

"Faith, why are you running away from me? Come on... stop. Hug me... talk to me."

"Go away!" I motion for her to be gone. "Leave me alone!"

"I will not," she says emphatically. Her friends follow us to the alley and stay behind her, a safe distance from me. "Let's talk—about whatever you want. Come on, Faith, let's just talk."

"Go back to Irony Heights! And leave me alone—you always have anyway!" I spit the words out as I walk away, trying not to trip over my feet, but a bout of coughing slows me down.

"Really, Faith? That wasn't my choice! I had to go."

I halt in mid step and turn to face her. "Oh, I know—'I couldn't help it that I'm a spoiled, rich brat and you're living on the street!'" My face turns into a horrible mask as I mock her. She presses her lips together and flinches this time, but doesn't back off. "By the way, you're interrupting my evening plans, I hope you know this."

"Faith." She ignores the hateful tone in my voice. Her hand slowly extends out to me. "Let me take you home. We've all been frantic trying to find you. Destiny is lost without you—she misses you so much." Tears are building in her eyes as she speaks, then they begin to flow down her cheeks. "We put up posters—called the police."

"Oh, well that makes it all better, Connie." I feel my throat tighten. *No! Do not cry! You will not!* "Maybe I didn't want to be found! Maybe I just wanted to come here and forget where I came from."

"But why? Because of Gran?" She moves closer. "Because of Mom? Did you come here because of Mom?"

"Yeah, I did—and I also came for me—to get away. To find something I didn't have at home."

Connie's eyes search mine, hungry for answers. "Please— God, Faith! I can't believe I found you alive and okay…you don't know what we've been imagining." Her friends in the back are crying now, too. *As if they give a shit about what's happening in front of them.*

"I can't talk now." I turn and start toward the other end of the alley.

"Wait! Faith, please wait." I stop but do not turn to face her. "You don't have to explain now; just come home with me."

Connie sidles around me to face me and swallows back her tears. "We can talk more at my place. Gran and Des will be so happy. Let me call them." Her hand touches mine, and I try to recoil but I can't. I feel a deep hunger for consolation, yet the pain and resentment I feel inside won't allow me to forgive her that easily. I draw my hand away and brush my matted hair out of my eyes, tucking it under my frayed and filthy toque.

"You really have no idea, do you, Constance! How can someone so self-aware be so utterly and completely clueless? You must really be submerged in your own selfishness right up to your asshole to not be able to see when someone close to you is drowning in misery and desperation." I cough again and wave her away. "It's too late for talking! You made your decision about me in your life at your nineteenth birthday party—*princess!*" The last word comes out in a raspy hiss.

"My nineteenth birthday? What are you talking about? You were there. We always kept in touch, saw each other all the time…we…"

My face fills with rage. "Kept in touch! You're my damned sister, Connie. And you're the oldest—you were supposed to fight for us, for me and Des, not abandon us!"

"I never abandoned—"

"Yes!" I shout in her face. "Yes. You did. And I wouldn't expect you to remember what happened at your nineteenth birthday party, because, of course, *cause* and *effect* don't even graze you; you remain unscathed. Why *should* you remember, right?"

"Stop talking in riddles and just say what's up your ass," she blurts, still in tears.

"Oh my God, stop, Connie!" says one of her friends. "She obviously needs help."

I look at her with what I figure is a horribly threatening glare, because she backs off right away and resumes her place behind Connie.

"Fair enough! No more riddles." I hold my hands up in mock surrender. "All truth now, nothing held back." Connie angles her head toward me, listening. "After you moved in with Josephine, Des and I could barely get the time of day out of you, and our visits happened less and less often, largely due to the fact that we had head lice and precious Princess Constance could not be near children with head lice. No, of course not. Nor is it about how we embarrassed you when we came over, and the last few times, Josephine had to drive us home early because you had a gymnastics competition or a fucking riding lesson." My pitch and sarcasm are rising with every syllable.

"No, that's just a fraction of the degrading ignorance on your behalf that I had to swallow as your sister. Oh, wait…I'm sorry…*half* sister. We can't forget the *half*, because you could not bear one hundred percent of my DNA—that would mean we were more the same than you want to admit. *My sista from another father but the same fucked-up mutha.*" I chime the last sentence with a rap-style delivery, hands in her face and all, feeling empowered beyond belief.

"You're rambling, Faith. Look, whatever I did, I'm sorry. Come with me to my apartment. I go to school here—I live here now. *Please,* come. Just for tonight."

"No. And I don't care where you live and go to school! Like I said, self absorbed is your middle name." I pause and breathe, feeling every muscle and bone aching.

"You have to know that I'm not going to leave you. I'll stay here with you if I have to, but I'm not letting you out of my sight now that I've found you. Just let me call Des and tell her you're okay."

"Whatever, I don't give a shit—but only Des. And don't try anything, or I'll just leave." Connie nods in agreement and starts tapping furiously on her cell phone. "And tell these bitches to go away." I shoot a twisted face at her friends, then turn and walk to a place behind some boxes just beyond the dumpster while Connie assures her friends emphatically that she is okay and that she will call them. In turn, they agree, on the condition that she checks back with them at the coffee shop around the corner, as they won't leave unless she does.

Wrapping my coat around me, I sit down on some cardboard, leaning against a wooden fence, and wait. I close my eyes again. All this activity has taken a huge amount of energy from my cold body and I need sleep. However, sleep has to wait, because Connie is at my side in mere seconds. She slides down next to me and wraps her arms around me. I welcome the warmth. We sit, silent for a long time, and watch the cobalt blue sky turn an inky charcoal. Eventually the moon rises, but still, she says nothing.

Every once in a while she texts as I watch, communicating with Des and telling her to wait and that I am okay and so is she. Then I realize how cold I am and that Connie is shivering, yet still, she says nothing.

*Just start from where it hurts, Faith, and let the words do the work. Let them come out like a sliver from an old and festering wound.*

"So, I'll just start from the beginning, I guess."

She nods, shivering. "Okay, whatever you want." Connie turns to face me and our eyes meet for just a second, and then she turns back to focus on the sky again, as though making eye contact with me might frighten me off.

"You know that for a long time you've been different—I mean, before I left Greenleigh." My gaze focuses on the scrawny bare limbs of a tree planted in a hole in the sidewalk down the street. "What I said before, about you changing after you moved to Josephine's? After awhile, like, I'm talking a few months after you went to your new school, you weren't the same. I don't mean superficial things like clothes or makeup, I mean mainly about the way you talked about Mom and Gran." I wipe my nose on my tattered gloves. "And even then, it doesn't really matter all that much to me what you said about Gran, but *Mom*—I mean, you never really came straight out and talked shit about her, but I know when your words are intended to cut someone down. And cut they did, over and over again, whenever we came to see you—and Josephine didn't help much, calling Gran all the time and yelling at her about the head lice. Shit. She would scrub my skin raw and pull at my hair until the nits were gone, but still, they came back again and again, I swear to God. I know that's kind of petty right now, but I've just always wanted to tell you."

"I'm sorry about the head lice thing," Connie says in earnest. "And maybe I did talk shit about Mom, but I was really pissed at her and I still am, in a way. She really fucked the three of us with her weak way of coping with life."

I can't disagree. "Yeah, but I was still a kid, you know. And hearing my older sister echo everybody else's opinions about the woman I wanted most to love me and care for me—did something to me inside. More than anyone else's, your words cut through me, Connie. The kids at school, Gran, our neighbors, Josephine—then you. It was like I was in a dark pit and slowly the walls were closing in on me. And when you started to get on Mom, I felt like I was being buried alive." My voice rises, as I remember the old pain. "It didn't matter when everyone else said stuff about her, but when you did, you made it true—then, deep down, I knew it was. That's when things started to get worse for me. I felt like everyone was talking about me and saying stuff about our family—or lack of one."

"Come on, Faith, we weren't the only ones with an abnormal family—I mean now, if you come from a family where your parents aren't divorced or separated, you're the abnormal one."

"Maybe, but it's not normal to have a drug-addicted runaway for a mom."

Connie pauses, and takes a deep breath. "That's true." She shivers again. "Can we get out of here and get warm somewhere? My apartment's about ten minutes away by cab."

I shake my head vehemently. "Not yet. I want to talk this out. Then *I'll* decide what I'm gonna do." I've become defensive again.

"Okay, okay. No worries." Connie blows warm air in her hands and rubs them together. "You know, Destiny is doing pretty good. She volunteers at St. Joseph's Hospital on weekends, when she's not working at the mall. And she won Gold in the district science fair last month—looks like she'll be going on to regionals."

"That's awesome." I have mixed feelings of great pride and jealousy.

"You wanna know what she did her project on? It's on drug and alcohol abuse."

I can't help it: I burst out in a huge snort of laughter.

The entire thing is just too ironic. Connie must agree with me because she's laughing, too. "Wow!" I manage to say when I find my voice again. "How very appropriate for her to score so well on that subject. She's been surrounded by textbook cases since she was a toddler." Connie nods, laughing softly.

"Actually, her research was brilliant. She used fruit flies and got them to develop a tolerance or something like that—"

"No way—that's incredible…." My voice trails off as I realize how people's characters and mental well-being can make them react to the same situations in polar opposite ways; I think of Destiny and then of myself. But then I think of Connie's situation again, and I know I can't let her get off that easily.

"I just had the freakiest thought, Connie. I mean, people respond so differently to their environment—you know, our family would make a brilliant scientific study. Our mother was a drug addict, who conceived three children by three different men, died as a result of drug use, and who I had only seen a handful of times in years; our grandmother is a miserable, neglectful old bitch who thinks that just feeding her grandchildren and telling them to bathe every week is the extent of her responsibilities as a custodial guardian—"

"Stop, Faith—"

"Wait, I'm not done." I'm getting angrier with every word. "Of course, it's the middle child who follows in the footsteps of her mother, she's mentally screwed up and living on the streets of Toronto. Then there's the youngest, who decides to use her knowledge of her messed-up family, hoping to do some good in the world. Of course, we can't forget the oldest child, who, relieved to be spared from living in a crappy house with an unfeeling grandmother, denies her siblings and may as well be living on another planet, and shitting in a golden toilet." I'm rambling and irritable and in need of a fix really soon.

"You know that's really an offensive thing to say, Faith." Connie gets up clumsily, shaking her legs to get the feeling back into them. As for myself, I feel the rage building. I can picture Connie at her birthday party, standing around with her shallow friends, acting like a queen bee, and thinking she was all that. I rise to my feet, too, egged on by the fresh adrenaline surging through me.

"Don't you call my words offensive, Constance! I heard you, goddamn it! You wanna know why I'm here, *Connie?*"

"Take it easy, Faith. You don't have to shout…" Her hands are up.

"Yes, I do! Because you need to hear it loud and clear! *You* are the reason I ran away. *You!*"

She motions to herself with both hands. "Me?" She shakes her head. "No, not me. *Don't* blame your inability to cope on me."

"Yes, you. Because *you* were all I had left. You were all the good I had left that was like…like *Mom.…* Someone to lean on, who I thought I could trust to be there for me. And then you just threw me away, like everyone else did."

"You're delusional," she says as she fakes a laugh. "I never did anything but support you. I made Josie drive to get you and Des until I was old enough to drive, and then *I* did—I came to get you or to visit. Don't lie to me about that shit."

I'm feeling really edgy now, and I note that there are pass-ersby who are gawking at us. The pain inside is starting. "You're so stupid, Connie," I say, clenching my teeth. "Your nineteenth birthday party…"

"Oh boy! Here we go again with the damned birthday party…"

"Yes, I'm gonna talk about your party because that's when I heard you tell your friends that I was the social outcast of the family." My breathing is shallow and I can't take in enough air. "You basically told your preppy friends that your sister is a loser. Now, in my books, sisters who truly care about each other don't talk shit about one another—am I wrong?" What is left of my common sense tells me that I need to calm down or I will pass out or something. Then my eyes well up. I try not to cry, but the emotion is too strong.

I can tell that she's thinking, replaying the night over in her mind, and as the tears rise in my eyes, I see the moment she recalls exactly what she said, where she said it, and who she said it to. Connie looks as though someone pulled a rug out from under her. Is she shocked that I heard her, or is she shocked that so few careless words could have affected me so deeply?

She folds her arms across her chest and looks down at the ground. The ensuing quiet seems to disinterest the gawkers, and so they move on, but now I can hear that her phone is blowing up—her friends must be wondering if I've killed her.

"Oh my God, Faith." She paces and turns her body in circles, as though trying to escape the truth. "I was drunk. I'm sorry, I'm sooo sorry." Her speech drawls out for emphasis. "If it's true that I did this to you—I just…" She shakes her head, her eyes finally meeting mine. "I'm sorry, Faith. I was just trying to be cool. I remember saying it to some of the girls from my school but I never thought you would ever—"

"You never thought I would hear you. By saying that you were forced to have your freak of a sister there, you absolved yourself from any voluntary association with me. But I was still at the party, thinking I was welcome." My tone is stoic, though I still have to wipe tears from my cheeks. My restlessness is increasing with every passing minute, and the pain in my bones tells me I need to get out of here.

"Again, I'm sorry, Faith. What can I do to help you? Please let me…"

"Nothing. Just say good-bye and go—go get your friends." I motion to her phone in her pocket. "They're looking for you—they probably think you're dead or something."

"I already told you I'm not leaving you."

"Look, I need to get a fix soon—so unless you want to come with me, that's where I'm headed next." Then the thought strikes me—maybe she *can* help me. I'll ask her for the money I need to survive the next few hours. I'm certainly not going to fall asleep in the cold, puking and convulsing. I need to get high again, and soon. "I feel really sick, Connie. Do you have any money you can give me? So I can buy some H."

"Are you nuts? I can't do that—that's like, enabling you—"

"If I don't get high soon, I'll get sick, Connie. Do you understand?" I shiver. "If you won't help me, I'll have to steal to get money for it." I turn abruptly to leave the alley from the other end, toward Gerrard Street, knowing that time isn't on my side.

Suddenly I feel a tug on the back of my jacket, and instinctively I whirl around and push her hand off. "What the fu—. Don't do that. I told you I have to—"

"Okay! I'll give you the money," she shouts out. Her breath is coming in short bursts. "I'll give you the money, just come with me afterward. Promise me."

I hold out my hand. "Give it."

"No. I…I go with you," she sputters. "That's my condition. I go with you, you get your fix, then you come with me. I have more money after that. I'll give it to you again, but you have to come to my place. You have to promise me, or no money." Her breathing increases. I see in her eyes that she's afraid. "Promise me or I walk away." The restlessness in my bones is increasing, and my head is starting to pound. I can't let this go too far; I've been down this road before. I'm ready to give in, though in a different way from my late-afternoon post-high grogginess. Connie's phone is ringing again.

"Okay. I'll do it. I'll come home with you."

My sister lets out a huge sigh, takes off her glove, and holds out her hand to me. This time I don't hesitate—I grasp it and squeeze it tight like she's thrown me a lifeline. A reaction I wasn't ready for on my part, but I never thought it would feel so good to let myself be overcome by someone else's hope against hope.

"Thank God, Faith. Thank God." She pulls me closer to her, and her arms wrap around me like wings. And then we just hug. We hug and cry for a long time.

Then Connie calls Des, and we cry again.

# Chapter 27

Connie was patient. She came with me the three times I visited Henry for my hits and stood outside uncomfortably as he ogled her from the window of his car in the back alley. Once my fifth set of folds was done, I knew I couldn't do it anymore—I was living for my next hit. Connie's conversations with Destiny and her "normal" way of life made me see it. That was when I approached Connie and I agreed to at least try to stop. She still wasn't exactly what I would consider my best friend at the moment—I was still cool to her, even though she was trying damned hard to be apologetic.

I lived with Connie for a couple weeks before I was ready to give up chasing the dragon. I told her about Shaylee and Taylor and Trevor and Kyle, and about the gentle kindness of Mrs. Lieberman and how her death affected me as much, if not more, than Momma's. To this day, I still don't understand why that is.

In that time, I spoke to Destiny only once. I didn't want to talk to my little sister while I was on H.

"Please, Faith, let me come there," Des begged. "I want to see you so much. I miss you—and so does Gran. I know you don't believe me but it's true."

I raised my brows, laughed softly. *Gran? I don't think so.* "Not right now, Des. In a while, when I feel better." *Oh my God, I sound exactly like Mom. That's what she used to say all the time to stall us. Am I that much like her? Am I going to end up like her in the end?* "I swear, Des."

Gran wanted to talk to me, too, but I couldn't bring myself to reach for the phone that Connie thrust at me. Eventually, Connie made up some excuse about me needing to sleep, and I think Gran figured out I wasn't in the mood.

The only other person I spoke to every day besides Connie was Josephine. Her calm voice grounded me with her talk of the garden she would plant this year and of the early perennials starting to bud.

We decided on a place I would go to for detoxification— the beginning steps to getting clean. The name of the detox place at the hospital didn't sound offensive or scummy at all— it was called the West Toronto Mercy Hospital Withdrawal Management Centre. It almost sounded like a bank. Josephine's doctor suggested it, along with a clinic that specializes in treating teens with addictions. I was to check in there after my initial withdrawal symptoms dissipated.

On the morning I was admitted into the withdrawal center, Gran, Josephine, and Destiny met me and Connie there. When Connie ushered me down the long corridor to the Medical Detoxification Services desk, I saw the three women from Greenleigh waiting for me—I assume it was a show of solidarity and moral support for my upcoming cleaning out, but when they got a good look at me, there was a collective gasp. Had I changed that much in the year and a half that I had been gone?

• • •

Destiny meets me at a run halfway down the hall and throws her arms around me, almost knocking me over.

"Faith—I can't believe I'm touching you," my little sister gulps between sobs. I hold on to her tightly, but tears won't come for me.

"I'm so sorry I left you, Des." My gaze drifts to my Gran. "So sorry." Gran edges over, keeping a close grip on her handbag. Destiny sees her and lets go. With a Herculean effort only my sisters and I will ever appreciate, Gran lifts her arm and side-hugs me for a brief moment. Destiny exhales, as though she's been coaching Gran so she would get it right and has achieved her one objective for the event. I smile slightly, then turn to Josephine. Her pancake face powder is streaked by her tears, and she dabs at her eyes from under her glasses.

"So happy to see you again, Faith." I get a big hug from her. She smells like Chanel No. 5. "We're all rooting for you." A smile warm enough to make toast graces her mouth, but I start to feel the slight cold of "need" coming at me.

I had my last hit about four hours ago, which made me feel relatively normal. But everyone knew that wouldn't last for long—about halfway into the intake meeting, I'm edgy and nervous and irritable. The need is coming fast.

We walk as a group to the admitting desk, and soon a nurse appears from a room down the hall. She has beautiful skin and pink lips. She shows us into the little intake room and has me fill out some forms. "I need a signature from a parent or guardian?" Her request sounds like a question as her gaze skips from Gran to Josephine.

"That would be me," answers Gran. She purses her lips as she signs and draws in a judgmental breath. Destiny's pointed gaze goes right for her, and Gran eases up.

The nurse asks some questions, then she explains the procedure to me. "All right, honey, so you are going to be started on what they call a medical detoxification program. This program will take place in this special hospital wing, where you will be closely supervised by trained professionals who will use medication to help you through the withdrawal process." She smiles, but I'm now distracted and breaking out into gooseflesh as I shudder with a chill.

It's time. Before I go in, I grasp Connie's arm and pull her toward me, holding on to her for what seems like forever. "I'm so afraid, Connie," I finally say, my voice a raspy, tearful whisper. "I don't know if I can do this." I sense she knows I don't mean only the detox, I mean everything.

"You are a tough, determined woman, Faith." She holds me like a mother holds her crying child. "You have strength and courage in you that you aren't even aware of. You're gonna kick ass." We all hug for a minute or two longer, even Gran hangs on clumsily, and then the nurse tells them that it would be best if they leave and that staff will be in contact regularly to let them know how I am doing.

"You never know how strong you are until being strong is your only choice." Bob Marley said that.

I'm whisked away and placed in a hospital bed, hooked up with an IV cocktail of medications to help me purge the heroin out of my body. The cocktail will also help to ease the physical side effects of withdrawal, such as vomiting and cramping.

If that cocktail is easing the symptoms, then I'd hate to feel the full impact—I think my head is going to explode. Think of your worst flu, your worst sick ever. Now multiply that by about a bazillion times and you'll get an idea of what detox feels like: shivering cold sweats, throwing up, a twisting pain in the belly that feels like someone is tying your guts into a knot. Throw in muscle spasms and soiling yourself a few times, and all the romance of drug use flies out the window if it hasn't already.

All this peaks at about Day Two then tapers to a dull, numbing pain by about the seventh day—probably due to the muscle twitching and dry retching. I feel myself slowly swimming up from the shadows, and I let my essence feel the sunlight again. But only a small ray will be permitted to peek through the layers just yet.

# Chapter 28

"Our treatment program not only addresses substance abuse and addiction, but also treats the underlying psychological and social issues that may be affecting your sobriety." My eyes are intensely focused on the counselor's eyebrows. *Underlying psychological and social issues.* She moves them in such a way that they're synced harmoniously with each syllable she utters. I'm finding it hard to concentrate on what she's saying about my "next step in the journey to sobriety" because of those damned eyebrows. She turns to Gran and Connie.

"We work with clients and their families to identify and target the possible underlying causes and vulnerabilities linked to addictive behaviors. Our approach here at Horizon House is to provide a foundation for long-term sobriety."

*I want some dragon*, I think to myself. *I want some of that curly white smoke.* A shudder and a headshake, and I'm back on her eyebrows, chasing the thought away by thinking of the hell that I just came through.

"Jesus, here we go again," mutters Gran under her breath. The counselor's smile falters just a hair at Gran's comment and then recovers nicely.

"Let's try and be positive," says Connie.

"Hmph." Gran then natters on about something to the counselor, at which time I promptly tune her out.

*It might be nice to have a routine again. It'll give me some-thing to do—almost like going to school every day, except I go to rehab.*

"Oh yes, family visits are important during this process and allow the resident and family to begin the road to improv-ing their communication and healing their relationships."

*Really need a hit right now.* "She'll have four weeks of inten-sive inpatient therapy, and then she'll come back daily on an outpatient basis, tapering off the visits the longer she's clean and sober." *Chase the curly white smoke.* "That's usually about ninety days, every day, then less and less as she needs it."

"Are there services for family here, too?" asks Connie.

"Yes, I'm glad you asked—and we cannot stress enough the importance of family for Faith at this time." *Is she talking about my family?*

"Horizon House provides counseling sessions to educate family members about the disease and to develop an under-standing of what Faith's needs will be when she returns home. By creating an informed support system, the chances that she will not go back to her earlier habits are increased. This also allows you, as her support network, to improve confidence in your ability to assist in the recovery efforts in a healthy way."

Gran and Connie nod in all the right places.

In the end, I am able to glean that I will also have home visits prior to discharge so that I can "have an opportunity to practice skills" I've learned and allow my family to see my progress and prepare for the transition for me to return home. *Sort of like a trained monkey,* I think.

Day One is spent in orientation and learning daily routines, having medical exams, going over rules, schedules, and being introduced to all the other freaks in the program.

*Don't know if I can do this.*

• • •

The next morning is the start of my first full day in rehab. I share a room with a girl named Lily, who looks like a baby prostitute. She's pretty quiet, which suits me just fine.

After breakfast, I go to my one-on-one session with Dr. October Common. He's one of the psychologists here, and we get an hour-long session every morning; he's been assigned to me. I like the way he looks—like Ice Cube in a button-down shirt and Dockers.

"Hey there, Faith. Pleasure to meet you." He extends his hand over his desk. I take it briefly, then sit on the puffy chair across from him. Dr. Common speaks to me about our schedule and about his expectations, and as he's talking, I'm looking out the window behind him. My gaze settles on an oak tree outside

the office, aflutter with robins and starlings. The robins are giving the bully starlings a run for their money. *Get those freakin'
birds*, I think. *Get 'em.*

"Faith?" The doctor moves his face between me and the
birds.

"Oh, sorry, Dr. Common," I say, looking at my hands
folded in my lap. "It's hard to focus."

He smiles. "No worries—it's perfectly normal. Your brain
has been through quite a bit in the last week or so. Probably
needs a break."

"Yeah."

"And call me Dr. October or just October if that'll make
you feel more at ease." *Will I ever feel at ease again?*

Then he starts with the rapid-fire questions. "How old are
you?" His pen is poised over his chart.

"Seventeen."

He starts scribbling. "Where are you from?"

"Greenleigh, Ontario."

"Family?"

"Two sisters and a grandmother. My mom is dead. Not sure
where my dad is. Last time I heard, he was in Saskatchewan."

He glances at me briefly. "How long were you using?"

"Not long, four, five months, but it was a huge habit."

He nods knowingly. "Must have been tough. But I've
treated people who have been using for years. You're in a good
position right now, Faith." I press my lips together and nod.

We finish our prelim session. Next is relaxation therapy,
where we learn about techniques to help us relax—duh. I don't

know about anyone else, but I can think of something that would help me relax right here and now. Unfortunately, chasing is not an option.

After that is lunch. A healthy lunch that tastes like grass and cardboard.

Some time in the library is followed by afternoon group session.

"Good afternoon, everyone," says a lady at the head of the freak circle group. There are about ten of us in this session. "I'm Elaine Newman, your therapist and group counselor. So happy that you have made the choice to embrace wellness. Wellness means overall well-being. It includes the mental, emotional, physical, occupational, intellectual, and spiritual aspects of a person's life. Incorporating aspects of the Six Pillars of Well-being model, such as choosing healthy foods, forming strong relationships, and exercising often, into everyday habits can help people live longer and improve their quality of life. And can stave off the cravings of substances that have become habit-forming." *Easy for her to say.*

She appears pleased with herself at this point, but I gather that everyone else is relatively unimpressed. "Tell us a little about yourself." Newman looks at the guy to her right.

I want to turn and run and not stop until my heart bursts because I'm jumping out of my skin. The Darkness inside me is back. Highlights of Day Two.

• • •

*Day Three. I hate this. Like I have to adhere to a script. If I say what I'm really feeling, they'll stick me back in the hospital detox wing for the rest of my life and throw away the key. Think of something insightful to say—think!*

We watch a short film on an exchange between a mother and her teenage son, which is incredibly tame compared to a lot of the exchanges I experienced with my Gran. It is on the first pillar of well-being, apparently.

"So the first pillar of well-being—emotional wellness or coping effectively with life's stressors and creating satisfying relationships—is exemplified in this scenario. Would you like to share how you feel about this scenario, Faith?" asks Newman.

My mouth and throat are dry, but I force myself to speak, my eyes on my shoes the whole time. "Uh, well, I feel like Robert needs to back off and chill." My response has a rote quality, but it's the best I can do.

She nods her agreement. "Good, Faith," she says in an encouraging tone. The others in the circle appear jittery.

It's the end of the third day—long way to go—can't sleep.

• • •

"Today's focus in group will be the second pillar of wellness—intellectual well-being." Newman's tone is well practiced. "In this, we will turn our attention to the importance of recognizing our creative abilities and finding ways to expand our knowledge and skills."

I think of my knowledge and skills, which I could probably place very comfortably in a thimble. Maybe that's not quite true—I must be good at panhandling, considering it supported a crazy heroin habit. *Think positive, Faith, you idiot, remember what she said—thinking positive will help you to realize your full potential and cope with the stresses of life.*

*I did look after Destiny all the time when she was a kid—shit, I was like her second mom.*

"Can we share a trait that we are proud of?" *Oh crap! Circle sharing time again.* "Who would like to share—Josh?" Josh is the nastiest asshole in group. He swaggers in every day, thinking he's better than everyone else just 'cause his dad owns a few coffee shops. *Big friggin' deal. You're an addict freak just like all us lowlifes.*

Josh arches his brows and takes in a deep breath. His posture says everything about him—slouched in his chair, legs sprawled out in front like all this is a waste of time for him. "Uh, I prefer to pass." Passing is always an option, but he says it so sanctimoniously, I want to throw a chair at him. That's when I felt the need bubble to the surface again. The craving. The want. The shadow in my core. When would it get better?

I listen to the others share, and then it's my turn. I bite my lip and pick at a hangnail. Reluctantly, I begin to talk. "I think…my best trait is…taking care of my little sister. Only she's not so little anymore; she's, like, nearly fifteen."

"That is a wonderful quality to have," says Newman. "Being able to nurture others is so important in your own recovery."

"You only have one sister?" asks Toma in his heavy accent.

I shake my head, my eyes downcast. "Two. One is older than me."

"They addicts, too?" scoffs Josh, a sick smirk on his face.

Newman looks like she's about to let him have it. "Remember our rules in group, Josh," she says firmly. "We respect those who have the courage to share, and empathize with those who don't yet have the courage to do so."

I feel vindicated but I need to tell them something. "It's not my fault that I'm here." The words shoot out like bullets. Josh lets out a big snort, after which Toma looks him squarely in the eye.

"Why you don't shut up?" Toma says.

"Really, it's not," I continue.

"Go ahead, Faith," Newman encourages.

"It's my big sister's fault—she made me feel like a piece of dirt. Like I'm not worth anything. That's why I ran away and eventually started using."

"How long on the street?" asks Toma.

"A year and a half, almost."

"Same time using?"

"No. I started using about a year in."

"What put you over the edge?" asks Josh.

"Losing another person I cared about."

"Then that technically wasn't your sister's fault, 'cause, then, it's like *you* couldn't handle it."

"Okay, I think that's enough. Faith was brave in sharing and we need to support her, positively." But as Newman speaks, I begin to wonder if what Josh said is true. *Is it really me? Was it me all along?*

"Tomorrow I'd like to talk about the next pillar, occupational well-being. In this we derive personal satisfaction and enrichment from work, making meaningful contributions to our community…" I drift off into my own disorganized thoughts as the counselor wraps up our session. My mind is swimming in a swampy soup of cravings, self-doubt, and angst, making me even more jumpy.

Wasn't this place supposed to help me? How is making me feel like this going to help? I don't want truth, I want to feel good again. My head pounding, I skulk off to my room to lick my wounds. Day Five is a bust—can't sleep.

• • •

"Is there anything you'd like to talk about today, to start?" Dr. October Common asks in his usual friendly tone. My expression is neutral as I rock myself in his plush chair. I shake my head and keep my eyes on the rug.

The doctor waits, then says, "Tell me how you are feeling right now."

I shrug. "Okay, I guess."

"Really, you feel okay?"

I shrug again and remain silent.

"How are you handling your cravings?" This is something I am barely able to cope with. The feeling of constantly wanting to jump out of my skin is getting tiring, but what is getting to me even more is the fact that I will have to fight this battle the rest of my life.

"It's really hard some days—actually, every day."

He nods. "Maybe we'll revisit your medications to help with that. I'll take care of that as soon as we're done here."

"Yes, please, and can I get something to help me sleep?" I ask. "Cravings are really hard at night." *It's got to get easier, 'cause if it's going to be like this, I'm not going to make it.*

"It will get easier, Faith, I promise you." His pen scrawls something on his chart.

"Will everything else get easier, too?" I surprise myself as I blurt out a question that's been chasing my thoughts around in my brain for the last week or so. "After I get out of here, is everything else going to get easier—'cause if not, then I'm doomed. I'm fucked if I end up in the same place. I might as well just leave here right now 'cause all this isn't going to do me much good if everything stays the same out there. I feel like there's an animal eating away at any happiness I ever manage to grab onto. It's inside me, dark and waiting…and I never know what it's gonna be every day. Angry, sleeping, taunting…the Dark is inside me, and it spreads into each of my cells every day. I see the cop fall on the Blood Porch, dead, his brains on the cement steps." Tears are falling but I don't cry. My hand cups my mouth. Maybe I've said too much.

Dr. October licks his lips. "I understand your fear and I'm glad you're sharing with me finally. Don't be afraid, Faith." He reaches across his desk, over files and papers and notes, and opens his hand. To me, it's like a bridge, crossing over all the crap from the past and maybe trying to help me get to my other side. I take it cautiously.

"I'll try not to be."

"That's a good first step." He sighs, almost with relief. "I want you to keep in mind that we will work with you and your family to give you the best opportunity for you to be successful in this. Once you complete this program, you will have tools to help you maintain positivity and good mental health. You will continue to receive help from us here; it's not like we abandon you. We'll help you to connect with others and stay positive in your recovery, and especially, you'll get lots of direction in developing coping skills in a healthy way. We'll talk more about the 'Darkness' and the 'Blood Porch' and try to get to the bottom of why you're struggling, Faith. It'll take time, but one of the best ways to do that, believe it or not, is by talking about it and, surprisingly, helping others." At that moment, I know what he says is true—I felt at peace and worthy when I was helping Mrs. Lieberman.

Day Seven. I feel the faintest glimmer of hope.

# Chapter 29

My next fourteen days consist of morning one-on-one sessions with Dr. October, where we talk about the underlying causes for my substance abuse and he guides me through self reflection and self examination. We talk about the Darkness and the Blood Porch, endlessly.

Group counseling in the afternoon is supposed to help us develop healthy habits for social well-being, emotional well-being—even spiritual well-being. As a group, we engage in mock social situations where we may encounter stress and/ or temptation and then discuss coping strategies. In between is physical activity and healthy cooking classes, sleep therapy because I can't sleep, meditation, and relaxation therapy. When I hear myself sometimes, I actually believe I'm starting to talk like one of the counselors.

Connie visits me every Sunday, but our conversation is still strained. Des calls me from Greenleigh twice a week, tells me she misses me, and I tell her "same here." She manages to get Gran on the line, and after a few dutiful exchanges, I tell her to put Des back on the phone so we can gossip about Danziger Crescent. I know that Gran and Connie have attended educational programs for family here at Horizon House to help them support my recovery. I also know that I should be thankful, but I still feel a stubborn resentment hanging on like a barnacle and that's not good. One of the first things we were taught was to give up our anger and forgive. That's one of the keys to recovery. But my emotions have a mind of their own.

I manage to get through the Pillars of Well-being all right, and the medication Dr. October gave me seems to be doing the job. My cravings are becoming less frequent and less acute. I'm even sleeping a little better. After I opened up about my fears and the Dark place, Dr. October spoke with Gran about what happened. We started psychotherapy for what he figures is a big part of my problem.

We work on relaxation training, positive thinking and positive self talk, assertiveness training, and thought stopping. Dr. October says that it all involves me changing my thinking. It's about talking and reliving and talking, almost like your brain gets so used to you talking about it, it's no big deal anymore. It's helped a lot, but I know I have a long way to go.

Then one day, Dr. October announces that I'm ready for my next step—a home visit. This is like a dry run to see how our dysfunctional family is able to cope and to help prepare for the transition—especially me, because, of course, I am the most dysfunctional one of the bunch.

The family agrees that the best place for me to be is Connie's condo. Since my visit is only a day, Gran will come to Toronto to see my progress. Of course, it starts off bad and gets worse.

Connie picks me up from Horizon House and we barely exchange two words in the car.

"Hi, Faith," she says as she ushers me to her new car. "How are you feeling?"

"Good. You know, better now that they have me stabilized and I'm in therapy." I peer at the interior of her new wheels. "When did you get this?" I ask.

"Gran Josie bought it for me last month. You never got to see it 'cause…" Her voice trails off. That's the end of our conversation.

We arrive at her condo and Connie deftly parks in her spot. We're both obviously nervous about the meeting, because the silence in the elevator ride up to her condo is deafening.

"Here she is," announces Connie as she opens the door to her place, trying really hard to be calm. Destiny and Gran are waiting for me. Des is slouched on the puffy chair that looks like a slipper, and Gran's perched on the edge of the couch. Destiny pops up and runs to me the instant I'm through the door.

"Hi, Des." We lock on to each other and hug for a long time. "Oh my God, I miss you," I whisper into her ear. I close my eyes and breathe in her familiar aroma in a way only a sister would know mattered. I caress her face when we finally release, and she sends a toasty warm smile my way.

"I missed you, too," she says. "You look great."

Gran gets up at her own pace and greets me clumsily with a quick hug. "Well, Faith, how are you feeling?" Gran asks, her chin up and her eyes looking straight into mine.

"Okay, I guess." *For a recovering addict*, I want to say it, but I don't.

She nods as she continues to survey me. "It looks like that place is treating you good."

"We're told that we are treated holistically; they look at the whole person and help us learn a new way of life so that we can succeed in our lifelong journey of sobriety."

My words have a purposely superficial tone because I don't want Gran to think for one minute that my recovery will make things easier on her. As much as every fiber of my being longs to be loved and cared for, I can't let go of the anger. Not done punishing them just yet.

I draw in a deep breath and I raise my brows provocatively at my grandmother, then I walk to the futon and flop down in a slouch. Des comes and sits beside me.

"So what are we doing today, family?" I say as I smile, though I don't let it reach my eyes.

Gran steps into the living room with Connie in tow. "We thought we'd just chat and then maybe have a late lunch," says Gran, straining to keep her tone cheerful.

I nod. "So what do we talk about?"

"Whatever you want," says Connie.

"Tell us about what they do at the rehab center," blurts Destiny.

"Des," chides Connie.

"No, that's okay," I say with a shrug. "We talk a lot. Explain how we feel, how our emotions play on our addictions, our family backgrounds, how that plays on our addictions." I glance at Gran and Connie. "And how that affects our recovery."

"That's it?"

"No, they do lots of other stuff—you know, teach us to eat healthy, how to relax, we even learned how to meditate."

"Cool!" chirps Des. "What are the other people there like?"

I think about my roomie and the guys in session. How fucked up we all are, battling our cravings and the catalysts that brought us there. "Good. Everyday people, like me."

"Any celebrities?"

"Nope. Just your ordinary addicts."

Des nods, disappointed.

"What about the other thing?" asks Gran. "How is that going? Is it any better?"

"The Blood Porch and all that?" I ask.

Connie shivers and squirms uncomfortably in her seat. Gran nods yes.

"It's actually helping. I talk about it a lot with Dr. October. He says it's the best way to deal with it. It's helping my sadness, too, but he says I have a long road ahead—I need to keep up the psychotherapy and keep using my coping skills. He thinks I can beat it without drugs." In point of fact, I am rather proud of myself.

"That's awesome, Faith," says Destiny.

"So great. Uh, I think I'll get lunch on the table," Connie says as she rises, looking a bit uncomfortable.

"It's in the oven, Connie—I'll help." Gran follows after her, equally uneasy. I look at Des with a glint in my eye.

"So talk to me about school," I tell her. Her face brightens when she hears I'm interested. She chatters on and gossips about her friends, how they can sometimes be great and then they can be immature, and how much she's looking forward to grade ten. All the while, I'm thinking how well she turned out, how peaceful she looks, grounded, smart, and confident. I wonder if any of her positive traits were due to my sticking by her when we were little, when she was growing and needed some small measure of stability. And then later, when I knew how screwed up our family was, but never let her know it.

"Okay, lunch is on the table—I ordered from a new place I found—healthy and fast, so we have more time to talk." Connie points to a chair. "Why don't you sit there, Faith. Gran, you there, and Des, here."

It smells good, making me realize I am hungry. We all dig in. Plates and forks clatter, water is poured into glasses, and bread is passed around.

"So the treatment really is helping you, Faith?" asks Connie between mouthfuls. "They told us you're on medication for the cravings and that you're sleeping better now."

"It was tough for a while." I nod as I chew on salad. My response sounds colder than I intend, which makes us fall silent again. We look at one another, uncomfortable except for Destiny, of course, with guilt weighing heavily on our ability to open up.

"I'm supposed to come in tomorrow, talk to your doctor," offers Gran. "It's a kind of assessment, but he wants to set up some appointments where we can talk together about all this."

"What do you mean 'all this'?" I ask.

"You know, why you ran away and why you took the drugs. He says that we need to talk about it together if there's any chance you're gonna get better—and stay better." Her words bounce around in my head like an echo. Did I just hear her right? I'm sitting across from her and she doesn't for once think to ask *me* why? She needs to wait for a family therapy session to find out? Never once has she asked me how I feel, how anything affected me, how she could have made it better.

"And that's tomorrow," I say stiffly.

"Yeah. Dr. Common said it's a joint session. That's where the therapist guides parents or guardians—"

"I know what it's about! I'm living it right now, remember?" I snap. I'm mad as hell. Now she wants to go for counseling? Where was she when counselors were calling her in elementary school, begging her to come and talk about stuff? Where was she when I wanted Momma so badly, when she was too messed up to look after us 'cause she had "raised her family"? Where was she when she should have moved us out of that shithole of a neighborhood because she knew it was nothing but trouble— case and point: her own daughter. Now, when everything has gone to shit for me and only me—she's all chapter and verse about family counseling.

"Family counseling," I repeat as I stab a chicken thigh with my fork. "You wanna talk to Doctor October about 'all this.'

I've been around a long time, Gran—why haven't you ever asked me about it?" Des puts her fork down and looks at Gran.

"Maybe I never thought to." My grandmother pushes the food around her plate.

"You never thought to?"

"Maybe I never wanted to."

"Yeah, I think that's more like it."

"We can find out tomorrow, when we talk to—"

"Well, I want to know now, Gran! I want to know!"

"Know what, Faith?" Gran's voice is even.

"Why is it only me? Why? Why am I so screwed up? Why is it—"

"Can't we ever have a conversation without you turning it into an argument?" interrupts Connie. "Can't you see she's trying?"

"Yeah, she's trying 'cause she's got an actual doctor up her ass, pressing her for answers as to why her granddaughter is so fucked! That's why she's trying, Connie, you self-righteous c—"
I look at Des. "Jesus, I can't even say the word!"

"Leave her alone, Connie. She's right," says Gran. "I dunno why. Maybe you fell through the cracks. Maybe I wasn't listening. That's what the doctor wants to talk about tomorrow."

"Maybe Connie needs to come along. She had her part in 'all this,' as you call it."

Connie wipes her mouth and takes away my plate and hers. "Why are you still so damn mad at me all the time?" she says, as she stomps back and forth from the kitchen to the table, clattering the dishes together like they had something to do with her being pissed off. "Yes, I'm sorry for the hundred and tenth time—I'm so fucking sorry again!" She pauses and breathes in deep. "But I was the one who scraped you up off the street. I was the one who sunk to street level for you, hailed cabs, and brought you to get your fixes or whatever you call them, until you got your shit together and decided to get sober."

"Oh my God in heaven," says Gran, clutching her chest.

"I was the one who took you to the hospital and then the clinic to get you clean, and you take every opportunity to throw it back in my face. Why do you insist on punishing me? Why! If it wasn't for me, you'd be dead by now. You would have let yourself freeze to death behind a dumpster in that alley." I sit calmly and wait until she is done. She is reaching a crescendo, and I'm not about to interrupt her with my version of my life.

"Maybe you would have preferred that I left you there, Faith!" She points to Des. "Destiny is two and a half years younger than you. She lived in the same house, saw and heard the same things, and she's not walking around with a huge chip on her shoulder. But you!" she bellows, then points her finger at me. "You have to make everyone else's life miserable, you have to make the same mistakes that Mom made and screw everyone else up with your anger and shit—you're just like Gran—full of hatred and resentment, thinking that everyone owes you something 'cause you've had a hard life. Well, get over it!"

Connie's chest is heaving as she paces across the small living room of her apartment and she has to gasp for breath.

"There are plenty of others who've been screwed and were able to pick themselves up and go on. It's time you did that, too—sissy!"

I pause, waiting for more. When there isn't any, I smile, then chuckle. I let out a huge snort followed by peals of laughter as I double over on the chair, the giggles ringing out in the little condo. Their faces bear a stunned look, and I'm certain they think I've finally snapped and lost it.

I laugh for a long time, Connie's words are that absurd to me. How smug of her to think she can preach to me. How perfectly self-righteous and utterly blind to think she has a single iota of an inkling as to what I—and Destiny—have gone through. My mind races as I think of my response, but I have to remember that she's a victim, too; a victim of our own family dynamic. *I need a hit so badly, I can almost taste it.*

"Okay, first of all, how dare you judge me. You have no idea what being screwed over feels like, much less having to pick yourself up, so do not preach to me. Second, you're damn right I have a chip on my shoulder because, contrary to yourself, I didn't have a childhood or adolescence to speak of. I had to be mother and father to our little sister, which is probably why she turned out relatively normal, as you call it. Once again, no thanks to you, because you were off in Pleasantville, playing princess. You stayed away, because it was too hard to face us when you'd come back—too hard to admit where you came from—too hard to acknowledge me as your sister. Too *easy* for you to just ignore us." I lower my voice, thinking about my words and the depth of the truth in them. Constance's eyes are welling up. "Instead, you let Josephine sway you into hating Mom, and then you saved yourself."

"She never needed to sway me. Mom did fine making me hate her all on her own. And I've come to terms with that. I don't hate her anymore. I see her as she was. But you—you're different, and I think that's what fucked you up. How could you *not* hate Mom. Look at what she did! She practically killed herself and left us alone."

"She was sick, just like I'm sick. But no one helped her. No one reached out to her."

"I helped your mom, but she kept falling back into the trap, into the same spider's web."

I look at Gran with little more than contempt. "You did the bare minimum," I say. "You never reached out to her."

"Oh, you mean, like I reached out to you?" Connie says, her angry words hanging in the air like a wisp of smoke.

"Let me finish!" I say firmly. "And third, *I* was the one who decided to get clean, *I* was the one who crawled back from the edge, *I* was the one who let you reach down and pick me up—because if I hadn't been ready, your pity would have been wasted on me." I swore that I would speak in even tones, to not sink to her level and shout at the top of my lungs. *Remember the strategies*, I think. I want a fold so badly right now, I smell the delicious smoke in my nose just thinking about it.

"You never know how strong you are, until being strong is your only choice." Bob Marley said that.

"No one is responsible for me, Connie. I know that now. I've learned that. I just wanted a little of what you had.

The drugs made me not feel that need—for a while, at least." Destiny nods in quiet acknowledgment, her lips quivering. She reaches out and takes my hand. "The drugs numbed the hurt and chased the Darkness away. Now I know I was weak, but again, that is my truth. Please don't make my truth less valid than yours."

I get up and pace. My sisters and grandmother watch me as I stride back and forth, like a caged animal. Have I punished them enough? Was I only punishing myself or was I saving myself from something else—was my counselor right?

"I think I'm afraid, Connie—I'm still afraid."

"Of slipping back into using?" she offers quietly.

I turn to face the wall as I close my eyes and rack my brain. What is keeping me from taking back my life? What is wrong with me? *Just open your eyes and say it!* "I'm sad because of the person I could have been, and now that I see myself as I am, I don't know if I can live up to my own expectations. I'm afraid that if I let myself hope, I'll be vulnerable again. Like with Mom—God, I miss her so much—and with you, and then again with Mrs. Lieberman. This is what scares me. If I let myself feel, something always happens to take it away. If I don't give a shit, I won't get hurt and maybe the Darkness will stay away."

"You can't live that way, Faith," Connie says. "It's not healthy. That's why you hurt yourself."

"I know."

"Help me. Help Destiny," Connie says. "Stay clean, stay in counseling, and take one step a day. Just put one foot in front of the other and keep your eyes straight ahead. Every day is a page, Faith, you just keep turning the pages." I wipe my tears away and wonder how many pages my book will have.

"I'll be here for you, Faith." Destiny's tears have subsided. "I'll never forget sneaking into your bed at night when we were little and snuggling, feeling safe."

"Every day is a battle for me. You'll never know what it's like."

"Just think about later on—a few weeks from now," offers Destiny. "Maybe you can come back home and I can look after you for a change."

My eyes stray to Gran, and in my mind's eye, I picture Danziger Crescent, Wheelchair Louie, and the usual parade of druggies at his doorstep 24-7. "I don't—"

"I don't think so," interrupts Connie. "She's staying here with me."

My head snaps to look at her in surprise. "I am?"

"Yeah." She glances at Gran, who is swayed—no big surprise there—but Destiny looks crushed. "School ends soon. I'll be available all the time. We can go for walks, all that stuff we never got a chance to do."

"Why can't she stay with us? It's so far!" says Des.

"It's just better for her. Closer to the clinic, to Dr. Common."

"And away from Danziger," says Gran.

"You come too, Des," says Connie. "In the summer, stay here with us."

Des gasps with delight. "Yes!"

I run my hands through my hair and wonder if Connie may be right.

"I guess so...look, I'm really tired right now, my head's spinning. I have to go back to the center. Gran, you're coming tomorrow, you said, for an assessment meeting?"

"Yeah. First thing tomorrow." She sighs and looks at me. "I'd say today was a good start in family counseling, wouldn't you?"

I laugh. "Yeah, it was great. Great that we didn't rip each other's heads off."

On the ride back to the clinic, I find myself agreeing with my grandmother probably for the first time. We were finally doing what most people call communicating.

# Chapter 30

Gran Dot and I sit across from Dr. October Common. He's cluing Gran in on some of the realities of us users' success rates. "One important aspect to remember, especially in the early days of recovery, is that relapse is a part of the disease. Not every recovering addict will relapse, but many will."

*Oh shit, I friggin' hope not—do not wanna do this again.*

"Now, Faith, this would not mean that the treatment program was unsuccessful. If it does happen, it means that you and your family will need to pick up and move on from the relapse."

"Oh no, doctor, it's not happening," Gran says firmly. "I lost my daughter to this, I'm not losing my granddaughter." I look at Gran, stunned. *What has gotten into her?*

"Faith, do you remember a conversation we had about a week ago—about one of your earliest memories? The shooting across the street on Danziger Crescent?"

The feeling in the back of my neck creeps back whenever I think about it. I wipe my hands on my pants and swallow dryly. *Think of the strategies.* I shudder and look at the floor. "Yes, I remember. I'll never forget that."

"How are you feeling right now, Faith? Give me words, only words."

I have to really focus to put my finger on it, but all I can think of is "Anxious. Sad. Darkness."

"All right, Faith. Look up at me. That image still haunts you when you think of it, am I right?" Gran's eyes are flitting from Dr. October to me and back again.

"Yeah. I guess it's always there. I mean, sometimes more than others, but...yeah. I still see it."

"I remember it, too," Gran whispers. "It was horrible. The kids were little. Cops came to talk to the guy living across the survey, and he just up and shot one of them through the door. The other cop got a round off himself; ended up shooting that crazy guy right in the chest." I feel my ears buzz. Listening to Gran recount the story is like watching it on a movie screen. "He had a strange name, too. What was it now?"

"Sinbad. His name was Sinbad."

"Yeah, that's right—Sinbad. Holy smokes." I can feel the doctor's eyes on me. He's watching me, how I react, what I say, and what I do.

"Are you thinking about that day, Faith?" I feel foreboding Darkness all around me.

"Talk to me about it," says Dr. October.

Gran's watching both of us now. "What is it?" she asks. "What's the mat—"

"Shh. Let her speak."

I close my eyes and let the gloom wash over me. "This is so hard for me," I whisper. *Let me chase the dragon.*

"I know. It's all right; it can't hurt you," the doctor presses. "Tell me."

"I think about that day and I know that I can tell you the color of Sinbad's shirt, how the older cop's eyes look when they put him out on the ambulance stretcher, where the blood splatters are on the sidewalk and on the wall in Sinbad's hallway, and how the back of the younger cop's head is missing."

"God almighty," Gran whispers. She puts a hand to her mouth.

"Momma saved me that day—I was standing at the window watching, and she came up to the bedroom and threw me down and lay on top of me so I wouldn't get hurt. I'll never forget that either."

"That may be it, Faith. Everyone has one pivotal moment, somewhere in their lifetime, where they can say, this changed my life. Is that yours, Faith?"

Suddenly it all comes to me. My life is a cycle, a sometimes small, sometimes large spiral. At times it veers close to the experience and other times not so much, but it is always there. My life circled that day. The worst day of my life and the best day. The worst day because I saw two people die horribly. The best day because my mother would have willingly sacrificed her very life to save me, crystallizing her devotion to me forever in my mind—and mine for her. I relive that day every day. It affects everything I did, everything I do, and only now do I come to realize it.

I am lucid and logical. Everything makes sense. It wasn't me—it was never me. I wasn't a freak. I turn to my grandmother and reach for her hand. "Mom threw herself on top of me that day. She would have died for me, Gran. That's why I can't blame her."

"I know she did. She loved you so." Gran's voice cracks as she squeezes my hand. "Your momma loved Simon, too, and when she didn't have him anymore, she needed to fill that space—it was just something that she couldn't live without. And though she never admitted it, that overwhelming need to fill Simon's space with someone else, well…" She shakes her head and looks down. "…it took over every part of her life. She tried to be everything she thought Simon would want, instead of believing that she was good enough just as she was. She loved you girls so much. You need to know that, Faith. Then, maybe, you can forgive her, and go on."

I feel them build and then the sobs come in waves, huge rogue waves that shake me to my core. I fall to the floor and put my face in my grandmother's lap, helpless, much like the toddler so many years ago, looking out the bedroom window at an arrest going bad. Gran cries, too. I've never seen her cry before. Perhaps this is a good time for both of us to shed tears for my mother.

• • •

"It's post-traumatic stress disorder, or PTSD for short," said Dr. October later that day after Gran and I had regained our composure. "It was never treated properly—probably wasn't even on anybody's radar back then, especially where kids were concerned. You'll need continued counseling and psychotherapy, but hopefully, now that you've been diagnosed, we can all work through it. This is good news, Faith. Good news."

# Chapter 31

Occasionally, I feel a visceral, deep pain bubble to the surface. A pain for which there are no words. I sense it flowing out of me until I feel a little rebirth. I will feel this over and over again in my life, of that I am sure. This pain will come in many forms: cravings to chase the dragon one more time; anxiety, like when I need to run, run, run away from the things I can't handle; crushing sadness, the animal in my stomach eating my happiness. It's life, isn't it?

"You never know how strong you are until being strong is your only choice." Bob Marley said that. And now I understand.

The pain will always come and go, and I need to recognize that and deal with it in my own way—never like everybody else, because I'm not like everybody else. And that's okay, too.

Time is racing on. Next week, I'm starting high school courses at a local adult education center on the advice of my counselor. I'll work on my diploma, on my own terms, on my good days, and work around my sessions. They are the most important thing in my life right now—besides my sisters, of course. Connie will continue university and go on to law school or whatever she ends up doing, and Destiny will no doubt win a Nobel Prize before she's thirty. And I will go on. I will take pride in each and every victory, each day of my life, and I will be the strong and courageous person I know my momma, my gran, and my sisters will be proud of.

I, Faith Emily Hansen, am happy with me for the first time since I can't remember when. I'm eating healthy, taking my meds, attending sessions, and soon I will start school. Yes, I think I'm allowed to be happy. I will keep writing and loving and struggling and turning the page to the next day, just like Mrs. Lieberman said I should.

I guess this is where the old-soldier metaphor comes into play—you know, the one I talked about at the beginning of this thing? Soldiers are at war, they struggle, get shot at, get hurt, and fight their battles. Maybe they get screwed up, but they have to keep on fighting—there's no other alternative.

I still need to talk and talk and talk about everything and share my pain and my joy—yes, I can feel that now. And I know that my talking helps others, and others talk and talk to me and give me their pain. That way everything is shared and passed around, and when that happens, the load is lighter and it's just easier to carry.

Call it distraction, call it focus, call it a load of crap, but that works for me.

Anyway, for now, this is my ending. I keep moving forward, because there really is no other alternative.

And I keep writing.

• • •

It's early morning right now, on a hot and brilliant Friday just before the Labour Day weekend. Destiny, Constance, and I are walking on the Beaches boardwalk, not far from the Mimi's Natural Grocer apartment where Mrs. Lieberman lived and died, and where I got hooked on heroin. My flip-flops are making a slappy sound as I walk, and I have my hands in the pockets of my jean shorts.

"Can't beat this, eh? I'm gonna miss this when I go back to Greenleigh," says Des. Her gaze shifts to the lake, where sailboats dot the smooth water.

"And I'm gonna miss you," Connie says, taking Destiny in a gentle headlock. "I'm so glad you stayed with us this summer. It gave us a chance to get to know each other again, right, Faith?"

"Yeah—hundred percent." My hand spontaneously finds Connie's and we lock fingers.

"And don't forget, Des, you're coming back in a couple weeks and then we are in Greenleigh for Thanksgiving," Connie says. Destiny nods.

"So, already second year of high school—that's, like, way too fast for me," I say.

Destiny scuttles around behind us to my other side and slips her hand in mine. She draws in a deep breath and asks, "So, you're sure you're staying here, Faith, and not coming back to Greenleigh?" Her eyes look at me pleadingly.

"Yeah, I'm sure. I'm gonna be fine. No, wait—I will be *well*—that's better." I try to think of how I can explain it to her so she can understand why I'm not returning. "Like, I have a really good doctor here who understands what I need. He helps me to see who I can be, you know? I think the only way to get through this is by believing that I have the potential to be someone...to do something...meaningful." I shrug. "Maybe I can even help others who are like me. That'd be a good thing, right?"

Destiny nods, and Connie sends a smile her way. We're swinging our hands in unison now, like we did when we were little kids.

"You're gonna be okay, Des, if your brain doesn't explode because it's too full of facts and things. And Connie, here, is going to be the next Amal Clooney. And I'm gonna be all right. We're all going to be fine." I smile at them, and we keep on swinging our arms as we walk out onto the warm sand.

# Afterword

I recently woke up with a gnawing sense of sadness, not knowing the reason for it. As my consciousness lifted from sleep, my brain ran a quick check of the events from the day before. Nothing. Again, I tried to muster some recollection of what was causing this lucid yet peripheral feeling of sadness and I realized it was the hidden sorrow in a distinct pleasure, *Breaking Faith*, E. Graziani's fifth novel. I thoroughly enjoyed reading the book and it was clear that the authentic characters and powerful depiction of social and individual forces had affected me.

The realistic portrayal of Faith, the story's protagonist, takes the reader right into her tragic life; one can't help but wonder if E. Graziani knew Faith personally. In speaking with the author, it becomes apparent that she knows hundreds of

Faiths through her career as a school teacher; and has felt the urge to right the wrongs—the seed for the book.

How do children become happy functional adults? The outcome depends on a myriad of interacting factors, some are determined before birth, such as genetic predisposition for certain traits, socioeconomic status of the parents, and maternal habits during pregnancy. Then comes the bonding between parent and child; attachment, dependability of the adults in a child's life, family dynamics, nurturance, protection, guidance, encouragement, etc. The author could not have weaved a better story with this multitude of factors, so true to the nature of life's unexpected and often unpleasant changes. E. Graziani's charming storytelling cleverly draws on the extensive research behind her book through a rich dialogue of wit, sarcasm, and eloquence, all, while evoking feelings of sadness and empathy for Faith.

As a psychiatrist who sees a lot of "Faiths" and their families, I was impressed at how the author was able to bring the clinical elements of the story together so seamlessly with the narrative. The successive unfortunate turns cumulate into crisis when Faith meets the dangers of street life, which are then juxtaposed with the warmth and kindness shown by Mrs. Lieberman. Stress and trauma are inevitable in life. While the natural outcome to trauma is not disorder but recovery and resilience, post-traumatic stress disorders are the result of the interplay between genetic vulnerability and social factors, manifesting in symptoms. This risk is increased if after the traumatic events, essential treatment and services are not administered.

Trauma can uncover inherent vulnerabilities. Alcohol and other street drugs have always occupied the age-old self-medication method of dealing with trauma. The harmful dysfunction of addiction hinders a person and their loved ones from living their lives.

The prevalence of these issues is on the rise, and the author's wish to increase awareness will certainly succeed. I am excited about the mental health educational value of this book, especially for the at-risk population. Stories that are relatable and enjoyable convey the message effectively. Faith's insecurity about fitting into her peer group, along with her defensive indifference and anger, her longing to be loved by her mother, and her need to be validated by her older sister, can easily apply to many of us. Graziani's *Breaking Faith,* tells a captivating story that will not only educate readers about the personal tribulations of mental health, but will also warm the hearts of all those who follow Faith on her journey.

Dr. Vimala Chinnasamy MBBS, FRCP(c)
*Assistant Professor, Faculty of Health Sciences*
*Department of Psychiatry and Behavioural Neurosciences*
*St. Joseph's Healthcare, Hamilton, ON, Canada*

# Acknowledgments

In tackling a book of this nature, I could never rely solely on my imagination or experiences to make it believable. I wish to thank and acknowledge experts and others in the know who facilitated and supported my research.

Thank you to City of Toronto Hostel Services and Children's Mental Health Ontario for their assistance.

Thank you to Katina Tzitzi, RN, and Lisa Woodrow-Steduto, BSW, for their willingness to share their expertise. I'm incredibly fortunate to have such supportive, caring and honest friends to whom I can run for opinions on my writing projects.

A big thank you to Dr. Vimala Chinnasamy MBBS, FRCP(c), for her guidance and contribution to this novel. Her caring attitude and thoughtful recommendations were instrumental in my being able to present *Breaking Faith* to my publisher with confidence in knowing that it is as authentic and accurate as possible.

Thank you to Kathryn Cole, my managing editor, for championing this novel (and for editing and reediting) and to my editor Kelly Jones for her careful eye to detail and subtle, yet vital suggestions. I hope we made *Breaking Faith*, the best it can be.

I could not have written this book without my past experiences as an educator. I love Faith—she deserves better, but often doesn't get a fair chance to show the world her potential. I love her often contradictory qualities, her loyalty, her cynicism, her rebelliousness and her ability to respond to kindness with kindness, though we wouldn't be surprised if she didn't.

# About the Author

E. GRAZIANI is a teacher/librarian, author, and speaker. She is the author of *War in My Town*—one of the Canadian Children's Book Centre's Best Books for Kids and Teens and finalist in the Hamilton Arts Council Literary Awards for Best Non-Fiction—as well as the 'Alice' young adult novel series, *Alice of the Rocks* and *Alice–Angel of Time*, and a novella *Jess Under Pressure* (Morning Rain Publishing). E. Graziani regularly speaks to young people about her books and the publishing process. She resides in Ontario, Canada with her husband and four daughters.

Visit her website: www.egraziani1.wix.com/egrazianiauthor